C. D. Grimes Mysteries
Book nine
Lab Test

Locked rooms are old hat. What about a locked security vault under 24 hr. surveillance?

(If you are one who feels Israel can do no wrong, skip this one. It was written at the time there were Israeli spies in this country and Israeli mercenaries training drug cartels in Colombia in guerilla tactics.)

<u>Critic comment</u>
<u>1989</u> The story was very good, the solution believable, and the style good. I am Jewish, so won't comment further or rate this one. I know CD Moulton, and know how he feels about extremists, and Zionists are extremists. I also know people much like each of those described in this book
– GGL

<u>2014</u> Interesting look at what was happening in 1989. A news story about Israelis training drug cartels in jungle warfare inspired this story, I believe.

We are taken from a report of a murder in a sealed and constantly observed vault in a genetics research facility. It seems impossible that it was murder, yet it is equally impossible that it was not.

Modern technology (of which part did not exist at the time of the writing) intervenes. International intrigue, in a minor way, is soon a part of the tale.

I feel this was far above the average works available.
**** HSSS

Contents

About the Author

CD began writing fiction in 1984 and has more than 300 books published as of 3/15/16 in SciFi, murder, orchid culture and various other fields.

He now resides Gualaca, Chiriqui, Panamá, where he continues research into epiphytic plants and plays music with friends. He loves the culture of the indigenous people and counts a majority of his closer friends among that group. He funds those he can afford through the universities where they have all excelled. "The Indios are very intelligent people, they are simply too poor (in material things and money.) to pursue higher education."

CD loves Panamá and the people, despite horrendous experiences (Free e-book; *Fading Paradise*). He plans to spend the rest of his life in the paradise that is Panamá

CD is involved in research of natural cancer cure at this time. It has proven effective in all cases, so far. It is based on a plant that has been in use for thousands of years, is safe, available, and cheap. He was cured of a serious lymphoma with use of the plant, *Ambrosia peruviana.*

Information about this cure is free on the FaceBook page Ambrosia peruviana for cancer. CD asks only that all who try it please report on its effectiveness on that group.

Lab Test

Prologue

Alma, my knockout wife, came from the bay dock on my Bonita Springs, Florida, property with little Scott, my youngest brat, hanging on her hand. Wilma Jones, the wife of a close friend who works for the Florida Highway Patrol, was a short distance behind her, walking with Dave, a friend who writes science fiction. Jim Barrow, my boatman, was washing down my Stamas at the Englewood dock while Paulo, my outside gardener, hauled the various items the women had collected onto a cart to bring to the house.

Lou, Paulo's wife, was off to Estero with her kids, Wilma's and my other one on some kind of visit. Cal, Wilma's husband, would be in around dinner time to share whatever feast Al was planning.

That takes care of about everybody who was there at the time.

Tony Jacobi, who runs the Crane factories (I own all those stupid companies – or fifty one percent, anyhow) for me would be in for the meal and would probably bring Shirley Bock, the girl who runs the private airport in Sarasota where I keep the jet, with him. He's been dating her ever since a case that.... But that's ancient history.

I was working in the medium house where I keep most of the Cattleyas and medium growers (I also have a very large collection of excellent stud orchids, a legacy of my late grandfather and grandmother. Gramps was the original CD Grimes, Detective, and Grams was the world-famous orchidist, Sheila Grimes. They'd lived in Nicely (God! I hate that name!) where I still maintain the estate and where Cliff 3 is running the branch of the agency. I also have a large orchid growing area there, though the ones here at Bonita and at my place in Englewood are no small items on their own).

I had a plant of Bc. Mike Nelson – Bc. Del Rosa "Lines" X Bc. Pastoral "Innocence" AM/AOS, my own cross – in my hand. Mike is partners with Shirley at the airport.

"That one's got fair form," Dave said, as they came to the door of the greenhouse. "You gonna have it judged?"

"In a block. I'm going to try for an AQ on twenty of them. They're all pretty good, but I doubt there's an FCC in the lot. (Dave raises orchids too.) Did you go out with Al and Wilma?"

"No. I just bummed around the mangroves in the Bassman.

"Have you noticed there are no fiddlers on any of those bay islands? I wonder why."

To tell the truth, I hadn't particularly noticed. Estero Bay is generally shallow so I hadn't spent too much time in the bay itself, opting to go out into the gulf and either up or down the coast to explore. There are far too many people in the bay. I told him so.

"Well, there's got to be some serious kind of pollution. I don't remember ever seeing places like this that aren't full of fiddlers. The water's dingy and silty too, so I suppose there's dredging somewhere. I haven't found much 'til I get toward the northern part of the bay, then I get into the Ft. Myers crap.

"Why don't you see where the problem's coming from? You've got the resources and are always saying you want to find useful ways to spend some of those billions."

He wasn't kidding about the billions, though I often wish he were. It was true enough I might be able to make some kind of change for the better. I would definitely try to find what was going on. I didn't doubt it was the direct result of some local political thing. The place is notorious nationally for its shady crooked political deals between commissioners and developers.

Cal drove up then and I noticed the amused grin that came over Dave's face for a fleeting second. Cal doesn't like him like I don't like Slats Lattimer, the coroner from the Englewood area. There's no real reason for the dislike, it's a chemical thing. Dave seems amused by it, which tends to irritate Cal.

"Cal's not supposed to be here for more than two more hours," I said. "I wonder what's going on? Surely they're not going to shift him already. He's been on this detail for less than a week! He always stays on a schedule for a month!"

"Maybe he has a case for you. He seems excited enough."

Cal was excited? How could Dave tell? Cal never looked any different than right now!

Dave went on toward the house, nodding to Cal as they passed, while Cal came directly toward me. "CD, I've got something that seems to me to be right down your alley," Cal said. "Len (Len Stewart, sheriff a bit north of here) said to tell you about it. Even Slats says it looks like your kind of thing. *They* sure as hell can't figure it out!

"Len's holding things pretty much as they found them for you.

"Al's going to hate me almost as much as I'm hating myself for putting off dinner, but you can come with me if you will. I can use the interstate and get us there pretty fast with the sirens. It's murder, so the excuse is legit. You *are* a state expert!"

I perked up at that statement. "Murder? My good old specialty! Lead on!

"Al! I'm needed in Englewood on a murder case!"

Alma sighed. She's used to being a detective's wife, so she knows this sort of thing will happen now and then.

"Even better!" Cal called. "It's another one of those locked room things!"

Now I *was* curious! I've had a couple of locked room

mysteries to solve, but they're usually rather simple. I have the ability to see things from an angle that clears up any mystery almost immediately. Most locked rooms are fairly obvious for one reason or another.

"It really *is* a murder and not something contrived?" I asked.

"Contrived? Really? A locked room murder that's not contrived? C'mon!"

I grinned and gave him the middle finger. "Someone wants to hang someone else. They commit suicide, while making it look like murder. There will be definite clues, in that case – all pointing to one specific person. I've seen cases where that was the way one person hung a blackmailer – almost literally. The turkey was as much as convicted and handed a death sentence when Cliff found the plans for the thing. The one who set it up and committed suicide tried to burn her plans in the building's incinerator, but the papers were so tightly packed the center of the bundle didn't even get very hot.

"That's what a lot of the detective business is, you know. Going through garbage."

"Not this one!" Cal shot back as we left the drive onto 41. "This one, they went to a lot of trouble to make it look like suicide, but ... it looks like a murder that was supposed to look like a suicide, but couldn't be because ... it's weird.

"Maybe it's another one of those things where somebody wants to complicate it so much we can't solve it. It would've worked very well if it weren't for the fact Slats Lattimer's the county coroner. He used some of the equipment you donated to them to show it couldn't have been suicide – well, that was obvious – but we can't see how it could've been anything else, either!

"This isn't going to be easy, CD."

I was really getting curious, now. "Oh, there's always some little gimmick that gives them away. Some trace under a window or door. Some glue residue, or a bit of putty. A fiber from a string where it shouldn't be. A scratch by a vent. Dust wiped off where there should be either none or a lot. Locked rooms aren't really very hard to figure, except in books."

"Oh? How about a sealed isolation vault inside a secret research laboratory that's underground with twenty four hour fully automatic surveillance, electronic foolproof locks and no way to use any vents or that sort of thing because there are none? How about when there was no one at the facility except for the victim? How about a hundred other little details – such as the fact the card for the vault door was in the victim's pocket, so no one else could have opened that steel door?"

"Then it was suicide with an attempt to make it look like murder. Back to that premise. I'll have to look over the setup. If it was in that tight a security area.... I just hope it's not one of those spy things!"

"Not likely!" Cal replied as he tried to get one of the rock trucks that were three abreast clogging the lanes at ten miles under the speed limit to move over. He finally went off along the emergency stop lane to get around them, pausing to turn on the CB to tell the drivers he had their numbers with an expert state witness along to testify to the fact they refused to yield to an emergency vehicle. They could expect very expensive tickets and a very sharp increase in their insurance rates.

He cut off the replies that started coming in whining voices and recorded the license numbers of the trucks on a portable tape recorder.

He then continued, "There wasn't anything there any spy could want. It has to do with genetic engineering, but not classified stuff. I think there was danger of a virulent lifeform escaping. That's what the secure vaults are for."

My first clue in the case was that Cal, Len and even Slats didn't know much about genetic research or they would have asked some very pointed questions. I keep up with the field.

I wanted very much to see that facility. Something smelled to high heaven – and we were still almost thirty miles away!

"I won't mention anything until you've looked over the whole place," Len said as he led me into the laboratory complex. "This is Ed Vore. He's sort of their specialist handyman and general gofer, but he also designed the security system. He's a bit of a genius about those things if the rest of the employees can be believed.

"He can answer any questions, but won't volunteer anything unless you ask him to."

I shook Ed Vore's hand. He was a nondescript, very average sort of person. That almost colorless blond hair, greyish eyes behind gold-rimmed glasses, thin, 5'10", a dull blue shirt with a pocket protector, pens, pencils, a thin calculator, greyish pants that were a little too large and tennis shoes. He wore a small diamond ring in a platinum setting and a cheap digital wristwatch on a plastic band. There was a neat little gold chain around his neck. When he spoke I was surprised at how well his voice was modulated. I had expected a whiny squeak.

"I'll follow you around for a few minutes, then leave you alone," he said. "It's really fascinating that someone found a way around my sec-system. I would have said it couldn't be done.

"Do you want to start at the, uh, the scene of the crime or somewhere else?"

"Let's start right here at the front door. I'll check it out on a direct path to the scene, then to any other place he spent a lot of time, then from all other entrances to the same places. I'll view the vault last. That way, I can make up any number of scenarios as I go. You tell me about the security as we go along. I'll ask Len about the time of death before I start so I'll know which parts to ignore because they aren't really that important."

"Slats!" Len called. "Can you come out here a moment?" Then to me, "We found the body, or Ed did, at four thirty or thereabouts. I'll give you part of the general background. The victim's name was Gus Eisingstein. He was doing research on genetic gene splicing. He was forty six years old, widowed, had two kids in their early twenties, was well-liked in a lupewarm sort of way and he worked nights.

"The readout on the door said it was opened at eleven twenty three and twelve seconds and closed nine seconds later – for the last time until Ed arrived. The sec system showed Gus was in his personal office until one and a half minutes before that and had been there since ten fifty one. He entered the lab building at ten twenty nine forty two."

Slats came up then and nodded curtly at me. I returned the nod in the same manner.

"One more thing before we go on," I said quickly. "Where are his kids now? Since yesterday?"

"Two. Gloria Lynn, daughter, twenty two, is in Cleveland, Ohio. Confirmed," Len said. "Kurt John, son, twenty, is in San Diego. Marines. Confirmed."

"Okay. Thanks."

"Slats, have you come up with a time of death?" Len asked.

"The monitor showed him drinking a cup of coffee and eating an egg and cheese sandwich at ten forty five. I did a quickie stomach content breakdown check that indicates he died somewhere between two thirty and three o'clock. Closer to two thirty. I'll do a deprivation test at the lab, but I'd say he died of a stab wound, wide-bladed knife with a blade at least seven inches long, entered the upper heart at a slightly down-ward angle and from the outside – left – with enough power behind it to cut the rib bones quite deeply. There was a round contusion over the right ear and a few contusions and abrasions around the lower neck in front.

"The knife found in the wound was *not* the murder weapon. The blade was too narrow and not long enough to have done the damage, thus the blade found was inserted well after death. As it was a small sectioning knife from the drawer in the bench, we can posit it was to appear the blade was the instrument of death.

"The wound could not, as I have explained, have been self-inflicted. It isn't possible a person could develop enough thrust at that sharp an angle – with the wrist twisted backward and outward – to cut into the hard bone in such a manner, much less for the victim to then exchange the death instrument for another. Death was instantaneous. The position of the body indicates that ... maybe Grimes will be able to deduce?"

I grinned. There wasn't any real animosity in such challenges anymore between us, though either one of us would be very glad to jump on any obvious mistakes.

"He was stabbed from behind by a person who was his height or slightly less. He was held around the neck by the left arm and stabbed across the body with the right hand. I would say the knife used had a knob on the hilt end which was first used in an attempt to stun the victim. Either that or our killer will have a lump on the left side of his forehead where he butted the victim.

"That explains the abrasions and contusions, as well as the wound.

"Eisingstein knew his killer, if the vault is anything at all like I imagine it to be. I'll have to check all that out later.

"That close enough to how you figure it?"

"Pretty much. I chalked out where the body was and took the sectioning knife away. Nothing else's been moved. Eleven identical knives in the drawer.

"He was six one and a hundred seventy three pounds.

You'll need that kind of information."

I nodded, then Slats and Len went back toward the lab while Ed and I went back to the front entrance. I asked him to show me how everything worked and to explain the safeguards.

"We each have an electronic key. This slot. You put your key for.... Here." He pushed a button to the side of the door inside and stepped out. The door closed.

"There's an electric motor inside the wall there that places four heavy deadbolts when the door is closed. If any of them don't fit exactly into place that light inside the screen flashes and a bell rings. Nothing will open the doors except the key cards from the outside. They can't be cut, jammed or other-wise forced. Titanium alloy."

"If someone had used a torch to cut it we'd definitely know. What happens if the power fails? Can't open the door until it's back on?"

"You can hook up any twelve volt automobile battery to the little box there (Pointing to a little steel box with a padlock on it), then use your key to open it. We all carry a key to the padlock. We've never had to use it. You have to have the key to the padlock with a comp code magnetically implanted that matches the code on the card. One person's padlock key won't work with another's card to open the door. If you unlock it that way you have to push it open manually, of course."

I nodded.

There was a recessed electronic eye over the door, which I noted.

"Does that cam work as soon as the key's inserted?"

"That works at all times. It's on a sixty hour recorder, dual cassette – so can go one twenty without changing anything. We run them for the sixty, then I scan them, save all indications of entry and reuse the tapes. Time is recorded on the lower lefthand corner of the screen. So is the date."

"If the car battery is used you won't have a record of who entered or left on that tape, right?"

"Separate systems on all sec recorders. Fully independent – and the codes on the keys and cards automatically records on the tapes. They each will run one twenty hours off of internal constantly recharged batteries. Built in. Tamperproof. If the camera's not working the door won't unlock unless there are *two* cards in the slot."

So our killer very definitely didn't come in or go out of that door.

Unless there were two in on it.

"Windows? Same safeguards?"

"No windows."

We went into the entrance hall, where we took the card out of the slot inside. The door closed, then Ed punched a complicated code on the two buttons and it slid open.

"Digital binomial access code," he explained, then waited for a question – but I knew perfectly well that any number could be written in binomials. Button left was one and button right zero. He punched: 10100011001100011110. I didn't know if the number represented anything that was supposedly particularly easy to remember, but I could use it anytime, now. He saw me watching and grinned.

"That's one hundred eighty six thousand two thirty two, or the velocity of light expressed in miles per second. Tomorrow, it's pi to nineteen places, then the square root of one to nineteen places, then back to lightspeed. If you forget and use the wrong one you have to know a correction code. I won't tell you that."

I grinned myself and waved for him to lead on.

"You can see there's a camera at each end of this hall. Same system.

"The third door on the left is Ed's office. The first is mine, the second is Ralph's – Ralph Meiner, president and general pain in the ass – Ed's, George and Nora Seely, security, records.

"On the right is the vault entrance and next to it the general storeroom and machinery to run the place. The only other entrance at ground level is at the other end of the hall. The cameras have automatic zoom lenses that are focused by radar. They'll move from person to person in three second jumps if more than one is in the hall at any one time, alternating at either station. They are activated to follow through various signals or by the trace in the badges. No badge, and there will be alarms and automatic isolation of the area.

"Out the rear door is a small entrance port to the parking lot. That's the one Gus used to come in.

"On the other side of that hall is the lab station where we grow whatever we've produced in the U-lab.

"Records are all in computer storage with connections to each office and lab, but we each use our own access codes so no one can retrieve anything someone else has input."

"Underground lab?"

"Umm hmm." He nodded. "Almost perfect isolation and complete control over conditions."

"I know. I have a greenhouse underground for that reason."

"Grimes! Of course! I've heard all about that greenhouse. Over on that tract you bought by the bay. We used a lot of the innovations from it when we built this place. Martinez did both your contracting and ours. He told us you designed the whole thing yourself."

I nodded.

"Same system in the back door?" I asked, and we went to look out the heavy titanium steel door onto a loading ramp. There were some small boxes on one corner and a Dumpster by the side down on the parking lot level. There were a couple of cars on the fenced lot.

We went back inside. Ed continued, "Same system all the way through. Same in the offices and stores. Same in the labs. Same in the vault.

"Mr. Grimes, no one went into that vault after Gus! It simply isn't possible!" He seemed genuinely disbelieving. "No one had entered the building after or immediately before Gus came in and no one left. It just didn't happen! They couldn't do it!"

"Someone definitely did. When Slats says it was murder, it was murder. If you have a murder you have a murderer. Gus was murdered in that room, ergo: Gus had that murderer in that room with him. Period!

"Now let's look in the offices and storerooms. I want to see if anyone could have hidden in one of those rooms."

"We can look in mine, which I have the key to open for us and in Gus Eisingstein's, which the sheriff opened with his key. We can look in the storerooms and labs, but not in the other offices unless we have Ralph and either Nora or George here to open their own."

"I see. Offices are strictly private, but you can go any-where else."

"Only Nora and Ralph can go into the roof lab. You can only get in with one of them. That's Nora's top secret place. She's working on ... a project."

"I didn't know you did any secret work here. What? Government?"

"Oh, no!" he cried, with a laugh. "It's secret only from an industrial viewpoint. She's working on a gene implant to make rice grow in salt water."

I thought about that. If there was such a process it would be worth billions to any number of countries – but then Ralph or Nora would be dead, not Gus.

"Did Gus do any of that kind of research?"

"The secret stuff? No. He did the lab work as to splicing

and isolating gene chains – that sort of thing – but he didn't do any of the secret stuff yet. He could have a lab built for himself if he came up with some new idea that looked like it would work and that would have that kind of value.

"We each have our own little projects. You know you've made the big time when you get a secret lab of your own! It cost over three hundred grand to put that lab up there for Nora, but even a partial breakthrough will make billions in return, so it's worth the investment. Ralph says fifty failures and one success and we've made a colossal profit."

I nodded again. *That* was getting to be a habit I would have to break.

We went to Ed's office, where he inserted his key but, unlike the outer door, it didn't open. A panel slid open and he punched a code on the two buttons, then it opened.

"Oh! I forgot!" he said. "The offices have an additional code. Mine's my birth date. The roof lab has two extra codes, plus the key."

The office was comfortable, having a desk, a sofa, a large library, file cabinets, a small refrigerator and stove, a television, a computer console and a private bathroom.

"The sofa's also a foldout bed. We sometimes stay for a couple of days – or the others do. If you get an experiment started that has to be checked every two hours for the next six days you can't run away. Nora and Gus are the only two who ever did that, so far.

"The other offices are about the same. We have the basic furniture and equipment, but we use it as we see fit."

We went to the security office, where there were a number of computers and twelve monitor screens showing the entire complex from inside. Two of the screens were blank. I pointed to them.

"Nora's private lab. Off limits, even for security, when she's in there working. Hey! That means she or Ralph is up there!"

He picked up a microphone under one of the blank screens and said, "Sec. Report. Who's on premises?"

"It's me, Ed. I came in to turn off the scanners in here while the place is full of people who might see something on those screens.

"Terrible thing to happen!"

"OK, Ralph. Did the sheriff see you before you went poking around anywhere?"

"He called me at home. I saw him and that coroner. The FHP man wouldn't let me come in without one of them along. There's an officer waiting just outside the door.

"I'll be down in a few minutes. I may as well write this up while I'm here anyway. Ten minutes."

We went from the sec room to records. There were rows of 3.5" floppy disks, each tagged with a colored tape with a code number impressed into the tape. There was a drive unit for the new CD technology that even Crane was still experimenting with. We've already been able to put more than fifty 3.5" disks on one CD! Tony predicts it can be refined to where it will store the data on as many as three hundred disks! That's nine hundred standard books such as these I write about my cases! They should be on the market for home use within ten years. I was impressed!

"I'll just do a quick pullout of one of my records so you can see how this setup works," Ed said. "I'm blue tape.

"This is dated March first through thirty one, eighty eight. It'll be a record of everyone who entered, what they did while here – or where they went, at least, and when they left."

He inserted the disk, then punched a few codes. March one came on the screen. I read the information:

6:19:47 Ralph Meiner, frnt ent, directly to office.
Keyed 6:20:12.
Remained inside of office until 9:14:32.

Telephone LCL 6:45:27 - 6:46:01
Telephone LD 9:10:19 - 9:12:43
Comp. trml ON 6:31:22 - 9:09:18
9:14:32 left office to roof lab directly 9:15:55.
Left R/L 10:34:16 directly to office 10:35:02.
Comp. trml ON 10:35:21 - 10:40:19
Telephone LCL 10:37:23 - 10:38:07
10:41:31 left office directly to front entrance.
Left building 10:41:57.

There was information on all of them. A delivery was made to the north side of the rear dock entrance by UPS from American Rubber Company at 11:23:36 with a notation that the invoice was listed and the material was in storage. Both items under code # ARC/ UPS:3/1/88-11:23:36GE.

"That's the source, delivery company, date, time and who it was for," Ed explained. "It was for Gus. There's a picture of the driver and anyone who came with him with the invoice. It would amaze you how clever some of those industrial spies can be, so we keep data on everything.

"I can bring up the file on that code if you like. It'll show the picture of the driver and the entire unloading process. It's all on this disk, so you can see the storage of all that detail doesn't take much room – but pictures take a lot of disk space."

"I know. I use computer storage on the orchids. One disk keeps records on all the plants at each range, but I don't keep pictures to disk because I could only put about four per three point five. I leave them on the video tape.

"You keep all phone calls?"

"No. Only when they were made and if they were local or long distance. There are recorders on each phone if you want to keep them. Same with the computers – just when they're in use. No data transfer, whatever."

"Can you show me everything you have from yesterday

noon until you discovered the body today? Also, why wasn't the vault lab checked before?"

"Sure. I'll bring up the tape and we can use trace to see what you like.

"I didn't know anyone was in the lab until I ran the tapes to record them so, seeing as no one had any projects there, no one looked."

I had an idea something vital was being overlooked in this. There was a screen that showed everything in the vault, so the body had to be in plain view on that screen from the time anyone entered the sec room. If that screen was out *that* would have stuck out like the proverbial sore thumb!

"This is – note the time and date in the lower left corner – twelve o'clock and one second AM. It recorded from the first second Nora was in the building, as were Ralph and Gus.

"Gus is shown in his office doing some paperwork, but the roof lab screens are blank, so Ralph and Nora were up there. I'll put a fast forward tracer, so it will jump to the next point anyone enters or leaves any particular place.

"There. Nora has come from the roof lab at one fifteen, goes down the hall to her office, turns out the light and goes out through the rear entrance and straight to her car at one nineteen and thirty seven.

"The trace works by following one individual from the point of movement until they leave. It's searching for her to return until now. Homes on a little ID thing in the badges we wear, but this system can trace on whatever traits we ask of it.

"There! She didn't come back, so it's now shifting to Gus.

"He left the office at one thirty one, went directly out the rear entrance to his car and left the grounds at one thirty four.

"It's tracing. Here he comes back last night. He gets out of his car at ten twenty seven, comes into the building at ten twenty nine and gets to his office at ten thirty, goes to the vault at eleven twenty three.

"It's tracing. I went into the lab at four twenty eight. It shows me entering there because I would then directly affect his position. He would be with me. You can see that no one else went into that room!"

"Why doesn't the thing show him in the vault? I thought you said everything was scanned except the roof lab?"

"It only shows the immediate area around the entrance door. The techniques can never be shown here because a spy could find them. His body was near the rear bench, so it's not on the scans.

"Mr. Grimes, *no one went into that vault except Gus until I found the body*! It would have shown in these scans – and we went through the entire scan recording to find anything at all!"

I said to go on with the records tapes, so he started the trace again. A delivery was made, but was left on the ramp beside the rear entrance to the left out of scanner range. It was picked up four minutes after six by George, along with another crate from storage that was put on top of it on the cart. There was a note on the crate to take it to the vault for Gus.

George wheeled two boxes into the vault and returned with an empty cardboard box, then went to his office.

Ralph came from the roof lab and left the building, then came in again for four hours during the day, then left until he came back to meet Cal outside the front entrance, then to talk with Len for a moment in the entrance hall, then to go with a deputy to the roof lab. It showed him coming down the stairs right then.

George Seely came about nine in the morning and spent from nine to twelve thirty doing inventory in the storage room, had a sandwich in his office, watched TV until two, then went back to the inventory until six twenty five, then left.

Ed came in at nine fifteen oh four, went to the back lab,

changed the tapes on the recorders, checked with George, went out from twelve thirty until two, came back, edited the tapes, looked puzzled, ran one of them back twice, then went to the vault and in. He came out running to hit the emergency call. Len and Cal showed up and went with him to the vault.

"You know the rest," he said. "I'll run the tape through on a trace of anything not covered yet."

A woman came to ring at the main entrance. No one answered and she left. Nothing else happened.

I noted that something wasn't in that record for me and really solved the case right then, but it wouldn't do me a bit of good unless I could supply a motive and method. It didn't make any sense.

"All I have to do is insert the tapes of the dates I want? I code directly from that to read the tape?"

"Uh-huh. You saw how I worked it. You trace by scanning until a certain person is onscreen, then punch TR with the control down, then scroll either up or down to use forward or reverse."

"Fair enough. I may have to spend some time here, but I hope not. Detective work is boring enough without this kind of tedious detail work."

I then went to the main vault to see what had happened there. It was a large room with nowhere except the door leading in or out. There was a circulation vent in the door, itself with a built-in fan, but I didn't see how that could be used to any advantage on an electronically-keyed door.

"This vault is as well-built as any bank's," Ed said. "The only way anything gets in or out is through that door. The vent for air circulation is routed through a maze. I defy you or anyone else to get anything in or out through that vent!

"The electrical is cast in the concrete of the walls – not run through conduit.

"If you don't need me anymore I'll go. I don't want to go in there again until I get over finding him like that."

I thanked him for his help and went in. There were glass cases along the wall to the left with special lights and temperature controls, tanks and cylinders of various shapes and sizes, hundreds of dials and meters, isolation chambers and all sorts of strange special electronic equipment, including a high resolution scanning electron microscope made by Crane (Me!). I was passing-familiar with most of the equipment.

There were benches around all the walls except for a space about ten feet wide in back where there was a stack of cardboard cartons such as I had seen UPS Delivering on that tape.

There was a large wide table in the center of the room with more equipment and four chairs set in little bays in the table top. There was a computer terminal at each bay as well as several microscopes and tools. All the benches and the table had drawers in an unending line. There were cabinets full of delicate tools and sterility chambers for many of those tools. I could see the smudges from the fingerprint boys all over things and wondered what the point could be. Anyone who could have been in that vault had a perfectly legitimate reason for having left prints there.

The chalk outline of where the body was found was in back near the stack of cartons between the table and the rear bench. There were various culture plates sitting to one side of the electron microscope and a cassette mini-recorder by a stool there – plus a notebook with various diagrams drawn on the top page. There was a red circle around a portion of each diagram and the notation, "IT!" by each of them.

There was a note that said "from Ecklonia maxima" at the top. I'd have to find out what that was. Probably a plant name.

There were several missing pages from the spiral-bound notebook in the wastebasket, but the diagram and so forth weren't complete on any of them.

I went around the room carefully but, other than the fact Gus had probably been doing an electron microscope studies of something, I didn't find much.

I went back to the cassette and ran the tape in it back, then played it. It was mostly incomprehensible to me except for when he mentioned the "responsive chain" several times in an excited voice. He mentioned "Ecklonia" a few times and "black mangroves" and "common traits with coconut palms" and various other such references.

OK. I had no doubt Ecklonia was going to prove to be some kind of saltwater plant. Gus was working on Nora's project or one very similar. He also had mentioned "Zea mays" a couple of times.

I thought a few minutes, then went out to find Len, who showed me the Polaroids of the body. He watched me as I studied them, then asked, "Solved it yet?"

"As for who, probably. As for how and why, no clue I can see. I'll have to do a lot of research with the records as well as along certain other lines. What was he supposed to have been working on in there?"

"*Supposed* to be?!" Len asked, perking up. "Ah! You *have* found something!"

"Maybe a small clue I can build on, but only if what he was doing wasn't what he was supposed to be doing."

Cal, who was standing toward the side, said he was supposed to be doing sections of some kind of bacteria that was being used as an insert mechanism on Nora's project – whatever any of that meant.

"It may mean he wasn't doing anything like that at all. I have to get home, but I'll want to come back here in the morning to work in the sec room and in the records.

"I still have to find out how this was done! There doesn't seem to be any way any person could get in or out of that vault without being recorded – so they *were* recorded!"

"I sorta think that, just possibly, the guy who designed the system could probably beat it," Len suggested. "If he couldn't, then this isn't murder at all."

"It really does seem to be tamperproof. I'll have Tony and a couple of the experts from the plant come out to find out if it can be beaten and, if so, *how*."

Len arranged for me to have full access to the records and security room as a professional expert working with the state and county police. I presented them with my full security clearance papers, even though there was no government work involved.

Cal drove me back home at a much more leisurely pace than we had made in going to the place. Alma had saved us both a hearty delicious meal, which we attacked with gusto, then went to the terrace with our cognac and coffee to talk about the bay with my author friend a bit. He agreed a study should be done of what was causing certain damaging effects in Estero Bay, then said he was going to drive into Sarasota to see his agent and to then head for a SciFi convention in New Orleans. He was going to exhibit some of his orchid collection in the local show there, so was taking some of mine along to enter for judging. He and Cal seemed to have come to some kind of truce, so it was a very relaxing and enjoyable evening, all in all.

As he got up to go, I asked him, "Dave, you research all kinds of things for your books and I know you've spent some energy on the plants in the bay out there to find what was happening.

"What are Ecklonia maxima and Zea mays?

"I already know what mangroves and coconut palms are. What's the critical connection?"

"Ecklonia? That's California kelp. Zea mays is Indian corn. I don't see any connection except they're all plants. Kelp is found under water, mangroves are direct waterline, coconuts are above waterline, but close, and corn is high ground.

"Kelp is alga. Mangroves are dicots, and corn and palms are monocot types. Maybe their differences are what's important? There should be some Salicaceae, which is a waterline plant in fresh water. Willows. Maybe a cactus or two to complete the list. Maybe a fungus of some type and a high altitude plant such as spruce.

"See you in a week or so!"

Those others weren't mentioned. Could it be the important fact was that they were *not* listed? What was it about kelp that was "IT!" in those diagrams?

He was working on gene insertion.

So that was it! I had motive! Oh, brother! Did I have *motive*!

Chapter two

I decided to wait until morning, then would call Tony at the Sarasota plant to have him meet me at the labs. If anyone could figure how to get in and out of that vault undetected, he could. He could also use his connections to find out a few interesting little facts for me. It was too bad he and Shirley left before Cal and I got back or he could have gotten some of it started already, but that's life.

I met Tony at a little Waffle House for coffee and to discuss some things before we went on to the labs. Len had gotten me a key and I was coded into use of the sec room, the records room, the vault, Gus Eisingstein's office and the storage area.

"I'll want you to go over the entire system with Ed Vore. He can show you all of it pretty well. I'll want to study some things in the vault, then in the office. I'll use the sec room and records after I decide how to approach it."

"It seems obvious this Vore character did it," Tony replied. "He designed the system with a little loophole for himself if he ever needed one."

"I thought so at first, but several things have changed. There's more profit in this if Ralph handles it. It could almost negate Nora's work. George would want to protect Nora for personal reasons – such as the millions that either one may get.

"I think Gus found the answer. I think he discovered how to implant a salt-resistant gene into corn. If he could put it into corn, it could go as well into rice."

"The rice could be grown directly in salt marshes, while the corn could be irrigated with salt water. I'll get a crew onto finding if there've been any feelers put out yet."

He went out to his car to use the secure phone he uses on

the government top secret crap work for the plant, then followed me to the lab. I coded us into the fenced parking lot, where we parked by the Dumpster beside the gate. We went in to find that Ralph and Nora were upstairs in the roof lab, but no one else was there yet. Another crate had been left on the platform to the left of the rear entrance. I noted it as Tony and I went in through that door. Something about that box sitting there started nagging at the fringes of my mind, but I didn't know what it was.

I showed Tony the setup and explained what Ed had shown me the day before about how it worked. I left him there checking the door and went to get the crumpled papers from the wastebasket, then sat to read the notes still in the notebook. I didn't find it to be very conclusive about anything, but then, I'm no expert. It did show me he had done quite a bit on Nora's project, then had suddenly drawn the diagrams I had seen the day before. That didn't make any sense.

I looked on the front of the spiral binder. It said there were 80 pages of lined paper inside. I had the four sheets from the wastebasket and counted 63 still in the folder. That left 13 pages of notes unaccounted for. Someone had gone to the trouble of removing those sheets and had carefully taken the strips of paper that were always left inside the wire spiral out except for the four pieces to match the sheets thrown away. I didn't doubt those 13 sheets showed in very great detail just what Gus had been doing.

Of course, anyone would quickly point out that maybe *Gus* had thrown those sheets away or removed them himself. I would have to find them in someone else's possession if I wanted to prove any different.

I turned the cassette recorder back to the start and listened to the entire spiel. More of it made sense, now that I knew what he was working on. He only turned it on to say things in a short criptic way. Many things were one or two words.

Mind association system. When I want to remember things I'll often attach them to a one or two-word phrase. It acts like opening file "LAB" on my home comp, which will bring up everything input about this case.

The other side of the tape was blank? When I played it there was nothing at all? He was recording over the side in the machine when they found it. It had been on that tape *and* in the notes. Our killer had deliberately erased one side of the tape – the side that had the goodies on it, no doubt.

Gus had been excited about what he was seeing when he made the part we found, but there wasn't anything there to really tell us very much about the research. The original work had been on the now-blank side of the tape. He was recording over stuff that was obviously, when I heard it, concerned with Nora's project. It was taped some time ago.

Tony was standing behind me, watching me stew. He had a little "bugchaser" device we manufactured at Crane X-Trends Div. for the government in his hand, scanning. He found all the outputs in the room as well as the computer connections and everything else that was broadcast electro-magnetically.

"No actual bugs, other than the door scanner. Find anything?"

"I think so. There are thirteen sheets of research missing from this binder and the side of the tape with his vocal notes on it is erased."

"Maybe he didn't use that side yet."

"He was taping over on this side. He would have simply turned the tape over, in that case – not rewound it to use the same side again."

The computer terminal suddenly said, "This is Ed Vore. I have a note to contact CD Grimes on my door. I saw you go in on the scanner tape. Push the blue button beside the microphone down to speak. If you want it left open both ways push the white one."

I found the button and said Tony would be right over to have a grand tour. He would enjoy talking with an expert in electronic equipment and security systems. They could trade ideas, as Tony was Crane's head troubleshooter.

"Maybe he can figure out how that system was ever breached. I've been awake all night trying to figure it."

Tony grinned and left while I went back to my notes.

I didn't find anything else there, so picked up the cassette machine and the binder with the thrownaway sheets shoved inside. I put them carefully into my briefcase and locked it, then spent some time with the electron microscope looking for what Gus had seen and diagramed that led to his death. I wasn't sure enough of what it was, so wasn't particularly successful, but I decided to take the slides in the case along with me. I locked them inside the briefcase and headed for the sec room.

Next project would be to go through all those tapes being made now while trying to find anything at all that would show less than normal consistency. I had decided that, seeing Ed could edit the tapes for the records, anyone else could do the same. It would be a matter of finding out how and where. If anyone *did* enter that vault – and they damned well had! – the fact had somehow been excised. I didn't know how to find it, but find it, I would.

More than an hour later Tony came in to ask how it was going. I explained that I thought something was removed from the tapes, but I didn't know how to find it.

"These are really sophisticated machines," Tony said. "I may be able to find what you want. All you have to do is tell me what you expect is there."

"There will be two segments taken off of the records of the vault's scanner. When the killer went in and when he or she came back out. All I can see to do is to watch the tapes in real time to see where there's a gap."

"There won't be a gap, in that sense. This stuff is on computer disk-type memory. You simply block the parts you want out, then push `delete block' to erase it. It's gone with no gap. The computer will put something else in that space on the disk."

"But the time will slip."

"Right! That makes it damned easy to find!" Tony said, pushing me away from the qwerty board. His fingers flew as he explained what he was doing.

"I'm going to have this thing trace the time only and to bring out any gaps of one second or more. There!"

He pushed the `install program' button, then the return.

Nothing changed for about ten seconds, then the screen rolled onto a frozen scene of the door to the vault.

Tony pushed the "up" arrow for a few seconds, then pushed the spacer bar. The scene rolled forward, showing nothing.

"Watch the time," Tony instructed.

...2:34:16 - 2:34:17 - 2:34:18 - 2:34:19 - 2:34:20 - 2:34:58 - 2:34:59 - 2:35:00 - 2:35:01.

"So our killer went in at exactly two thirty four and twenty one seconds. Now we scan forward to see when he came back out."

There was only the one gap. We checked the tape over five more times, but there was no other gap.

"That means the killer stayed inside that room until Ed found the body?" Tony asked. "That's not possible! The tape was edited after the murder and before Len got here."

"Then that was obviously when the murderer *left* the room. He was already inside. The same argument applies as to how he got in, but we know when he left."

"But he had to have been in there since before Gus went in, regardless. Why ... how? That's hours!"

"Why? Because he waited until Gus finished some very valuable research. How? I don't know. I may have a bit of an idea, though. I have to check out a few things.

"What happened with you and the genius?"

"They're *all* geniuses," he answered dryly. "Any one of them has enough savvy about the system to have thought of something. I don't put any of them out of it. That system is as close to perfect as any I've seen and is better than a couple I've designed myself. Ed's free enough with his ideas and was interested in the bug chaser. He wants to get one and set it so he can find anyone who comes in with any hidden transmitting or recording devices on their persons. He's not too worried about cameras because he can spot them pretty well now. The thing's not classified, so I sold him three of them."

"Let's find the gaps in the other tapes. Then we can check another idea or two and go."

"I see. There have to be gaps in the hall tapes and in the office tapes cleared until the time our killer left. He then returned legitimately and excised the records."

We found it, for all the good it did us. The killer had simply gone out the front door at two thirty seven forty one AM – a few seconds removed from each of five tapes.

"Anyone could have done it," Tony said. "They were all in this room at one time or another when no one else was present."

I nodded, then went to the records office while Tony went out to go back to the Sarasota plant. He would call me in the evening with any information his operatives came up with.

I wasn't able to call much from the records. I didn't have the codes for that stuff, but Eisingstein's extra work wouldn't be there, anyhow. I had to find out who knew about his research, how they found out about it and what they had done with the notes.

The more I thought about it, the more certain I was the killer had taken a tape recorder in there and had copied the cassette material before erasing it. That copy and the 13 sheets of notes from the spiral binder were carried out with him.

I had to put him in that vault, too, but I was more and more certain I would discover how that was done.

Something was still wrong. I was sure there was a lot more missing from that record than we knew. There was some way the sec cameras had found out what Gus was doing – or was it a matter of something he left in that vault?

I went back down to sec to study the tapes for awhile back. It seemed anyone who was using the vault would do the cleaning. Each was shown at one time or another taking a bag of waste paper or broken equipment, used culture plates and other stuff out and throwing it in the Dumpster – after shredding anything made of paper in the records room.

OK. He had left something in the wastebasket and someone had found it. They had added two and two – and found it really *was* four!

Weak. They couldn't know he actually found anything that way, only that he had an idea. They would then have to do a bit more research.

I checked the records again to try to see who had suddenly started dropping in when Gus was in the vault. They all did, but there was a signal when anyone used the keys that would give him plenty of time to conceal whatever he was doing. They were constantly in and out, regardless of who was already in there.

Those tapes were all edited already, but I couldn't see where anything was left out.

I leaned back and stared at the monitor. If I only knew what questions to ask it would give me the answers. I knew it!

There were a number of .EXE programs that were used

with the machine. I wondered if anything would come up if I programmed the computer for another mode.

I pushed "escape" and waited, but nothing happened except that the menu for the program in use came up. I punched F1 for "Help". It gave a commands menu. I read the menu and pushed [ctrl] [Q] for "quit".

The screen scrolled to DOS. I typed "INDEX", punched [ENTER] and a readout of the disk came on. There was a little box that said that 632,768 bytes were used and that 97,344 were available on disk. A second box said that 632,768 bytes were used in one item.

That was the file of tapes – but it gave me an idea.

I put another disk in and punched the "open file" spot with the mouse. I got the box like the one before that said 422,357 bytes were used in one item.

The next was much the same, but the next said 421,761 bytes were used in two items. I pointed the mouse to "index of files" and punched the button.

TTP 419,683 bytes : file 2/21/88

TRD 2,098 bytes : file LMTD 23,298 bytes

bytes available : 308,331

Program TTP was the one used for the scan records. I looked through the disks, found program TRD, inserted it, programmed the computer with it and instructed the machine to load file LMTD.

FILES MARKED LMTD: Limited access files

LMTD files are encoded and require a password for entry

See manual

RSTR files not accessible without proper codes

See manual

Damn! Classified material was handled the same way at Crane. There simply was no way to get that information without the code.

There were entries on sixteen disks going back sixteen

months. I thought then that only Ed could have put that stuff on those edited disks, but I realized I was sitting here and could put my own information on any disk I chose with any program I chose and with any secret code I chose. Anyone could come in here and could do that. Gus might have saved his records like that. He might have put that stuff on the disks himself.

He hadn't been working on that project for any sixteen months, but he might have been doing it on other things. I would have to ask Tony if he could come up with a way to retrieve that encoded information. For now, all it did was add another thing I had to find. There was enough of that already.

I had to get the killer inside the vault as the most important point yet. Without doing that I didn't have a case, short of the killer telling me how that was done. Even if he came up with a process to make corn, wheat, rice and oats grow in salt water there would be no proof unless I could find those original notes in Eisingstein's voice and handwriting. He could claim he worked it out himself (or herself. I mustn't forget that). Everyone here was qualified to do it. It did no good to know who if I couldn't prove how.

I could get the killer *out* of the vault. I'd already done that much.

Everything was in these machines and everything was damned well going to stay there unless I found the code.

I sat back to think for a long time, but couldn't come up with anything, so used the phone there to call Len. I told him we'd found the way the killer got out of the vault and that Tony had made a copy of the proof.

"Got *out*?!" Len cried. "What good is that if he didn't get *in*?" This was a joke between us. He knew I'd find a way.

I then sat back to consider that I had met exactly one of the people working here. Ed Vore had shown me around the place. Ralph Meiner's voice had been on the response one time and I had seen Nora and George Seely on the tapes. Ralph had been in the roof lab when they arrived and Tony talked as though he had met both Nora and George.

I looked over to the bank of screens and saw that Ralph was at his desk using the comp terminal and George was just coming in from the back lab. I watched him go to Ralph's office door and say something.

The roof lab's screens were blank, so Nora was still up there if Ralph hadn't blanked them because I was on the premises. Fair enough.

I got up and went down the hall to Ralph's door and knocked, though it was open.

"Come on in," he said. "I've been expecting you. This is George Seely.

"Find anything yet?"

Ralph was a rather large (obese) man with thinning black hair – obviously dyed – and a sharp hawk nose. His eyes were a deep penetrating green that may have been contacts. He was seated, at the time, but from the tapes I knew he was about five nine or ten and maybe two ten.

George was brown-haired with a good bit of silver-grey at the temples, five ten or eleven, one seventy five and was rather handsome in a magazine model way. There were reading glasses in his pocket, which I had seen him wearing on the tapes, but only when actually reading or working with the comps. He was sitting on the sofa.

"Quite a lot, actually. Nothing at all, in another way. We know how the murderer got out of the vault, which will be important when we discover how he got *in*!"

"How did he work that?" George asked.

"Very simple, really. He or she simply walked out of the vault and out the front door. He came back during the regular hours he worked and erased the few seconds from the tapes when he was leaving the vault, going along the hall and leaving the front."

"Then he would have done the same thing to enter," Ralph said.

"But he didn't. There's only the one set of excisions on the records."

"You haven't had time to watch the whole lot of them in real time," George said. "You just missed it."

"Oh, don't be an ass, George," Ralph said affectionately. "Grimes set the comps to trace for any breaks in the time sequence. No doubt, he's run through the entire records a dozen times."

"I guess you can do that, can't you?" George replied. "I'm not so much concerned as to how as I am as to why. It's disturbing to think that maybe Nora or I know whatever it is he was killed to shut up – unless it was for a personal motive of some kind.

"He was working on Nora's research, you know. I record and relegate all those results, so I know it all."

I decided to drop a bombshell on these proceedings to see who would blow up.

"Oh, I found the motive right away," I replied offhandedly. "Gus found the gene to transplant himself and on his own. It was something from Ecklonia maxima. We'll know who did it when we see who comes up with a process for sale. The killer took all the notes and copied the cassette Gus kept – or the important parts of them. He may have been brilliant in discovering a way into that vault, which remains to be seen, but he was stupid to take those notes that way. The binder says there are supposed to be eighty sheets in it right on the cover in one inch letters. To erase one side of the tape when he was recording over on the side left in the machine wasn't the brightest thing to do, either. What I want to do is find how he got inside there. It's inevitable he'll be caught."

Ralph was staring at me with a thoughtful look while

George was spluttering. Nora said, from the doorway, "I heard the last of that. So good old Gus actually did it! That's wonderful! I always said he had the brains and skill to beat me to an answer.

"Ecklonia? Yes, I suppose that's reasonable.

"So tell me. Did he confirm the process with cross-referential mapping, or is that in the missing notes?"

Nora was actually a rather beautiful woman. She was in her late Forties with that reddish-brown – auburn, I think they call it – hair that has the texture and thickness to make you think it's miles deep. Her eyes were a clear golden brown, perfect teeth and a dark, almost Latin, complexion. She had a very good figure and was about five eight and a hundred twenty pounds.

"Mangroves and coconut palms. I think he may have inserted it into Zea mays. I'm extrapolating from the bits we found, but it seems to fit very well."

"Zea would be easier. It could be irrigated with sea water. That would solve a lot of problems for a lot of people in a lot of places.

"The way this place is set up it wouldn't profit anyone here to knock off anyone else over any such thing. We're all equal partners. Since no one *not* here could have done it, one of us is going to head for Israel or one of several other countries who will pay a flat billion dollars for the thing and will guarantee safety to the person bringing it."

"Israel? They're our allies! They would never harbor a murderer!"

"What? You don't read the newspapers?" George asked cynically. "They have *spies* operating against us right here! They and any number of our so-called allies would sell us out fifty times over for something like this. The Soviets or China could solve a lot of their economic and food problems with it overnight. Even Japan could put something like this to very profitable use in a very short time. The only way to catch whichever one of us did this is to get him before he can get away."

"I'm afraid I agree," Ralph said. "Gus would have taken it right to Israel and would have given up his part of the profits on it. I'm Jewish, but I wouldn't give Israel the time of day, the way they're handling their problems now. You'd think we would have learned something from the Nazis. Israel seems to be using them for a model of how to treat people.

"I won't get started on that soapbox, Nora. Don't look at me like that. Gus and I would argue by the hour about it, but we weren't either one involved, so our answers don't count for much. I'll just say it's easy to sit across an ocean and condemn, but it's as easy to sit in the same place and excuse.

"I agree with Nora. Our culprit will run. He has no choice."

"Who will run?" Ed Vore asked from behind Nora. "What's this? A convention?"

"Mr. Grimes found that Gus found the answer to the salt-resistant genetic insert," Nora replied. "That means the protection as well as a lot of cash. Obviously, he'll run."

"Gus ... someone...! You mean?" Ed sputtered. "But ... but, I mean, none of us would kill him if he found the answer! It would mean we'd *all* be millionaires!

"Maybe the killer would rather be a personal billionaire and to hell with the rest of us," George replied. "Do you realize that one of us here in this room right now is a coldblooded murderer? It has to be one of us to have used the sec comps like that!"

"The sec comps?" Ed asked. "How did you...? He used the sec comps? I thought my system was foolproof!"

"There's no such thing as foolproof," I said. "I read an SF series called *The Flight of the Maita*. There's a detective, a robot, in it who notes now and then that for every new advance in technology that will thwart a crook there's a corresponding one that will allow the crook to use the same system to escape being caught. The comps were used to excise a few seconds from the tapes when the killer left the vault and went out the front door. He came back to work at his regular time, found an opportunity to go into the sec room and erased those few short seconds. Simple."

"Of course!" Ed cried. "All you'd have to do is scan the time sequence to find it. I should have thought of that. The only real risk would be if someone looked at the screen records while he was *in* there before he had the time to erase anything."

"The odds of that are nothing," Ralph said. "We have to be very careful until one of us runs. We're all in danger, now. We might remember some vague little detail – someone we saw in the hallway or in the sec room or something."

"The safety from that is for each of you to tell me exactly what you saw and when. The danger is only if the information can be kept from me by killing one or more of you. This killer won't hesitate. We're going to know who he is sooner or later, anyhow, but he has to buy time. I don't need to tell you you're all going to be watched at all times.

"I don't have the authority to make demands, but I'm sure Len will point out that no one is to leave this county until further notice. To decide to take a vacation or trip now would be very unwise if you're innocent and just plain stupid if you're not.

"I'm going to look around at a thing or two and will be gone, but I suppose I'll be back.

"Whichever of you is the killer here, you're exceptionally clever. I very strongly recommend against thinking that clever and intelligent are synonyms. Be careful you don't outsmart yourself – if you haven't already.

"Ralph, may I use your phone?"

"Certainly! May I suggest, as we're to be watched anyhow,

that our watcher be most evident at all times? I would personally prefer that an officer be right in this office with me at all times or by my side when we're not in the office. It will save the taxpayers money if he rides in my car and shares my home when I'm there. I'm a coward! I freely admit it!"

"You're the only one here who couldn't have committed the murder, yourself. Your girth makes it as much as impossible for you to have stabbed him in that manner.

"I'm not saying you couldn't be an accomplice, though that wouldn't make much sense. It would still bring about a split in the funds."

He grinned at me. "Well! I've finally found an advantage to being grossly fat! I mean it about the officer."

"Well, it's to be expected, I guess," Ed said. "I don't have anything to hide. Just about everybody uses the comps in the security room. It's sometimes a little easier than using the ones in the personal offices."

"I don't mind, either," Nora said. "If we can get the notes Gus made there won't be any reason to keep the roof lab so secret anymore.

"Mr. Grimes, could you give me everything you have that Gus left? I would like to – I have to – work with everything – and it *is* the property of this company."

I called Len, who would send the tails right over. Ralph spoke with Len about it while Ed and George went to the outer lab for something. Nora looked a question at me. I suggested we go to the sec room, where she could copy anything I had. There wouldn't be any point to keeping any of it from them. The killer already had the important parts.

It took almost an hour to go over everything with Nora. She said the most telling part of it were the diagrams left by the electron microscope. They showed he had actually made the splice.

"Wait! The comps!" she suddenly cried. "We can look at the scans directly from the scope! Come on!"

We as much as raced to the vault, where she coded the scope. We watched as the screen showed the whole thing as Gus had made the observations – or what the scope was showing him.

"He did it! He really did it!" Nora cried. "The gene's spliced into the Zea mays already. It'll be in embryo form, so we'll have to put the embryo into a seed and plant it. We can begin finding that part immediately! He'll have meristem-cloned the embryos if he was working with them like this."

"You know which plates have the embryos?"

"If I have to I'll plant every embryo in this lab into Zea seeds! If we can find his notes they'll be listed. Save time.

"We can go, now. There's nothing more to do today."

We went out. Nora went to Ralph's office, so I headed for my car. George was putting the heavy crate left on the rear loading dock onto a cart to move it inside. Right at that moment I knew the answer to one of my major questions. What had been nagging at my subconscious fell into place.

Now to find what I was missing in this. I knew the entire process and I knew the motive. I knew everything – except which one of them did it.

I don't really kid myself that way. With all of that I didn't see any way it could fit. What was missing was personalities. *None* of them would kill Gus for anything so stupid as a billion dollars instead of a hundred million.

Chapter three

I was talking with Len explaining what I had found and what I hadn't. I'd stopped on my way back home, both to report to him and to see what, if anything, Slats had come up with.

Slats hadn't found anything unexpected.

"Now for the good part," I said after we both had our coffee cups refilled from the pot that's always on the corner of Len's desk. Alma makes the blend for him, so it's the best coffee in the Englewood area, with the exception of the Harde Luck Cafe, where Leelah uses about the same recipe for the special.

"I know how the killer got in."

"In and out, then," Len replied. "Tell me how and we'll see what difference it makes."

"He was carried in there by George Seely. It means we can figure the angles as well as the killer did.

"You remember watching those sec tapes? Remember the crate on the ramp marked to be taken to Gus? Remember how George slid the crate onto the cart, put another on top of it from the storeroom, then took it all to the vault?

"The crate was set to the left of the ramp. The camera doesn't cover that little spot, but it seems to be where the UPS truck always drops off the stuff.

"Ralph said they deliver the crates at night, according to an agreement. The driver has a key to the outer gate. The killer simply slipped back into the crate after ostensibly going to his car and out. George always clears the ramp before he leaves. Simple enough."

"That ramp is smooth concrete for almost eight feet from the side. I suppose that's why there's no camera at that spot. Not likely anyone could climb it – and it's inside a locked fence."

"What finally tipped me off was the fact the container the shredded paper is kept in was against the side of the ramp yesterday, but was moved across the pavement against the fence today. Apparently, that's where it's supposed to be. The killer rolled it out to where he could climb on it and onto the ramp. He got in the crate around five thirty or so, waited for a little while in the crate, George took him into the vault where he could get out of the box and hide any number of places inside the vault until Gus came to work on his little experiment. The crate was small enough to where it was a little cramped, but big enough that a person could stand being in it for a good while. You could see it was heavy by the way George handled it.

"We may have to wait for awhile before our killer makes his next move. He can't take the chance of trying to sell the process now. It's automatic `GOTCHA!' time if he does!

"We can prove how he got in and we can prove how he got out. We've established motive and opportunity. The process is worth a billion dollars and guaranteed safety from the law here.

"There's one little thing in our favor, though. Nora will use those embryo cultures, so he has to move fast or she'll sell the process before he can act."

"He'd make millions anyhow. It seems such a totally stupid waste."

"It's greed. We've got it figured now."

The phone buzzed and Len picked it up. He listened for about a minute, shook his head a few times, grunted, raised his eyebrows at me and fidgetted. He hung up and said, "Well, there went the motive!"

"What's that supposed to mean?"

"That was one Nora Seely on the phone. It seems she went to her car to go home and found thirteen sheets of spiral-bound paper and a cassette tape on the front seat. Guess what they are!

"She did have the good sense not to touch them in case there are prints."

"We know that George and Ralph aren't the killers. I don't think Nora is, either. I thought Ed Vore was our number one suspect at first and I think so again, now. He's all that's left for it to be."

"George is out of it? Why?"

"Easy. He didn't push himself into that vault on that cart. Ralph couldn't possibly strike at that angle with his gut holding him back so far from Gus."

"I think maybe Nora Seely's our number one suspect. Stealing the process wasn't ever any part of it. Gus had stolen it from *her*! She gets millions, no matter who comes up with the splice, but now her great reputation as a scientist is secure.

"Ed Vore doesn't have the stamina to have gone through with it. The time in that box and the time waiting with Gus in that vault with him would have made him chicken out halfway through. If he did anything like that he'd do it spur-of-the-moment or not at all."

"Regardless of all that we're left pretty much without any motive, now. You can take the lab boys out there to dust the pages and listen to the tape. I'm going home, getting a good night's sleep tonight and going trout fishing in the morning."

He sighed heavily and stood. This would keep him up half the night.

I checked the answering machine as soon as I got home. There was a message to call Tony at Crane in the morning – he wouldn't be available tonight – about some strange new developments. Dave had called from New Orleans to say my plants were all entered in the show there. There was a call from Cliff at the Nicely agency that I returned. He wanted to tell me he had completed a case there for the big Crane plant and that two of my cousins from Hawaii had been there at the estate for two weeks. He sent plants to New Orleans from the range he was handling and Dave set them up as part of the Grimes exhibit.

One of the plants sent was Pot. C. D. Grimes, one of his own crosses (Slc. Orient Amber X Blc. Nicely Gold) that was blooming for the first time. He was going to come down to visit on his vacation (!) in a couple of weeks.

Alma came in to suggest that we go to Miritello's for dinner. That sounded good, so it turned into a pleasant evening. She asked about the case while we were eating – something she never does – so I told her what we had. She said it was probably Nora Seely – trying to protect her "Firstest with the mostest" reputation – then said no way, it was probably Ed Vore because George would have noticed if Nora hadn't come home until that hour, then said there had to be someone else because it didn't make any sense, no matter how you sliced it, then said it was easy to see why she wouldn't make much of a detective.

When we got back home there was another message from Tony saying he wouldn't be contactable before noon the following day, but I might like to check on the backgrounds of some of those people – particularly the two silent partners in the laboratory – and why someone hadn't bothered to mention there *were* any others.

He did that to keep me on my toes. It would drive me crazy trying to figure out what was happening that he knew and I didn't about *my* case.

I went fishing with Jim Barrow in the morning just to let Tony know I wasn't buying into the mystery bit. It really WAS eating at me, but I wasn't going to admit it to him or to anyone else. We managed to get back to the house ten minutes before noon, no easy trick in Estero Bay at low tide, cleaned the catch and had lunch. Dave called from New Orleans to tell me Pot. C. D. Grimes had taken "Best in Show" and had also been awarded an FCC. Cliff had certainly decided to name a good one after me.

I called Tony after lunch to find he hadn't yet returned to the plant, so I called Len.

"CD? Could you stop in next time you're close by? Maybe this afternoon?"

"What's up?"

"Two and two equals seven point four three one," he answered in a very strange and sour tone. "Nothing adds up here. I think you should see these papers and listen to this tape. The one that was on the other side of that tape in the vault, I'd guess. There seems to be someone else involved in this and I can't figure who! Gus was up to something. I think he may have been a spy, but I can't figure why anyone would spy on a stinking little lab like that."

"Because if they find what they're looking for it could feed a huge population, make drought a big `so what,' so far as food supplies are concerned, make or break the economy of almost any third world country and for a few thousand other little reasons. Tony's already suggested there are silent partners in the laboratory. He wonders why we weren't told about them – and so do I. I'll be there in an hour or so."

We talked for another couple of minutes, then I called Tony's machine to say I'd call again after I got to Len's office and found out what the hell was going on there. Alma grinned and raised one eyebrow when I told her the simple little locked room mystery case was getting complicated and I might be late getting back.

"Just don't get shot at. You're hard enough to live with when you're not wounded."

I drove on down to Len's office to find he wasn't there.

He'd gone to the labs. It seemed Ralph Meiner's body had been found in the shredded paper box.

On my way back to the labs I began to wonder if we really were involved with spies. I'd had some experience in that sort of crap and didn't like it at all. It was too easy for some foreign agent to come in, kill a few people and get out before anything could be done about it. Our own government would use anyone we caught to make some stupid "deal" with the worst offending countries. It was a political one-upmanship game to them.

Not to me, it wasn't!

Nothing was yet moved when I arrived at the lab. Slats' van was parked close to the shredder box, which was about four by eight and four feet deep. It was on rollers and had a pair of lids that dropped to stay closed by their own weight. It was one of those Dumpsters the truck drives up to, slides a pair of forks under, then dumps by swinging it over the cab of the truck, where the contents are dropped into a compacting unit.

Len was standing over to one side talking wth Ed Vore and George Seely. The crime lab crew were going over the grounds with a fine tooth while Slats was in the Dumpster with a cameraman showing him exactly where and at what angles he wanted pictures.

"The list of suspects is shrinking. Rapidly," Len greeted. "We'll finish out here and I'll want to get your ideas about some things.

"George Seely came out to dump a load of shredded papers about half an hour ago. He noted the blood on the lid when he lifted it, so looked inside. He called me and stayed out here with Ed to see that no one messed with anything until I arrived. You can get the facts about what's inside from Slats, but it's obvious he wasn't killed here.

"Ralph hadn't been seen today and his car isn't around. That wouldn't be unusual, except for the killing of Gus, so everyone expected him to be in early.

"We're going to check the sec room, but Ed says there wasn't anything unusual on the tapes – or anything that had caught his attention in a quick scan.

"Anything else will have to wait." That was asking me to shut up until we had a chance to talk.

"Let's see what's on the sec tape, then."

The four of us went inside and back to the sec room, where we checked all the tapes since everyone left the night before until the present time. The gate was opened at 5:18 AM, and again at 5:23 AM. The approaching car's lights were right into the camera from the front while the windows of the silver Mercedes were darkened. They showed nothing inside from the side cameras. All we saw was a red flannel sleeve that reached out to insert the card into the gate lock to open it.

"That's Ralph's car," Ed said. "The readout says it was his key card that opened the gate both times."

"It looks like the only thing I can say is where were the two of you at around five twenty this morning?" Len said.

"I was in bed with Nora," George answered.

"I was just in bed," Ed replied. "Did you notice that driver had on leather gloves? Does that mean it won't do any good to find his car?"

"Not at all. Maybe someone noticed a silver Mercedes somewhere in the early hours," Len said. "We have to find it. There may be any number of clues left around or in it, but I won't depend on it. I'll send in an officer to take your statements."

I walked outside again with Len. He sent Gibbons in to get the statements, then we went to the box, where Slats was climbing out.

"I'd estimate, without any particular evidence, that he's

been dead for about eight hours," Slats said. "Probable cause of death is a deep throat laceration that severed everything in his neck except the spinal column. He wasn't killed here. Probably half an hour plus since death before he was dropped into that box.

"There's a bit of what we call Florida peat in his shoes on the left side, indicating he was dragged. There's some decaying plant material there too, but it will take time to identify it. There's chlorophyll stain on the lower pant leg on the left side, another indication of dragging. There's water soaked into his socks and on the lower pants legs and there's a bit of what I would probably call small brown pea gravel in the cuff of the left pant leg.

"I found some grease stains on the back of his coat and along the right arm. There was also what appears to be a bit of road dust – mixed chirt, clay and sand with some oiliness.

"That's about it for now. He met someone who cut his throat. I'd say he was at a new house or one where they're doing some landscaping. He was dragged to the car, thrown into the trunk, brought here and disposed of. It would take a very strong person. He wasn't a featherweight."

"CD will agree with all of that," Len said. "For once you figured the scene faster than he did!"

"What happened to the cop you had following him?" I asked.

"When Meiner was home for the night and wasn't planning to go out again Forbes went home. I don't have the budget for twenty four hour surveillance when the subject promises he's going to stay put. In Meiner's case, the cop was there for his protection, so he took his word for it.

"Hell! He even said Lt. Forbes could stay in his guest room!"

"The others about the same?"

"Yeah," Len said bitterly. "They were all home for the

night by eleven."

"Maybe the killer's not one of these three. There are at least two silent partners involved in the business. We have to find out who they are. Ralph might have been killed to prevent our finding that very thing. Nora couldn't lift Meiner. Neither could Vore."

"Let me finish here, then we'll go back to my office," Len said. "I think you might be very interested in that tape Nora found on her seat. It proves there was someone in that vault when Gus made the notes on it. Voicecoder says it couldn't have been any of the people we have here now. There are two new voices at two separate times. I'd like to have someone to compare, so we'll have to find those partners."

I waited about half an hour for Len to get away. I sat in my car and studied the situation carefully from all angles I could think of and kept coming back to a foreign agent. That seemed the only logical explanation for part of it – but no spy would have left those notes in Nora's car! The more I thought of it, the more confused I got.

I followed Len back to his office, poured a cup of the coffee and read over the 13 sheets of notes and diagrams. They spelled out very clearly exactly what he had done with the gene splice.

"Nora says there's no doubt he completed the work," Len said. "She's got the codes for the spliced material and is implanting the embryos Eisingstein left into corn seeds right now. Nothing as minor as finding the bodies of her business partners is going to be allowed to distract her from that.

"I don't think she cares one single solitary damn about the money. She really is thrilled that Gus was able to make the major breakthrough. There is a problem with whether or not the result will be edible, but they have a base to work from."

I finished the sheets, then turned to the voicecoder machine on Len's desk. He ran the tape back a bit, then showed he had taken a voiceprint for Gus from that side of the tape. He then rewound the tape and put it into the machine. He took out a list of numbers.

"I have the inches where we'll find what we want, but you'd better listen to the tape for the whole side. Maybe you'll catch something I missed. It's a two-hour tape, so this side is an hour."

"I'll spend the time. I'm interested in this thing."

I listened to a lot of rather disjointed little bits of random information for fifteen minutes or so, but was able to follow it because of the diagrams and notes on the sheets. I was really absorbed in it when the first voice came very faintly into the background. It was a low baritone and was speaking from enough distance that only a few words were clear. Len was keeping an eye on the counter, so stopped the tape.

"That's the first of the voices. We took a computer enhancement from the voiceprint copy. This is what we have. The computer cut everything else out for us."

He turned on another recorder that was attached to a computer and to the voicecoder. I heard "... do these ... to it all? I don't ... well enough to ... (scraping sounds of a chair being dragged. Len said that was too loud to cut out) Try another angle on it. You don't seem to understand tha...."

"That's all on the first one," Len said.

I turned the voicecoder back on. About five minutes later during what was obviously another time in the vault the second voice, one slightly higher in pitch, came into the background. Judging from the radical changes in subject matter of the notes it was fairly easy to tell when one session ended and the next began. Len again turned on the computer to give: "... to back out of the ... not very smart. You don't ... do it!"

That was all in the other voice. There were only the two. I finished the tape. I had been jotting down a check mark every time there was a subject change on the tape. I had thirty one.

"We were also able to enhance part of the background residual from the other side," Len told me. "A fairly close estimate of the time when the first visitor was in there, checking back with the nights Gus worked in the vault, was forty to forty five days ago. The second visitor was about eighteen to twenty days ago.

"You said Tony told you there were two silent partners in this setup? We found one of them. Carson Wilder. Investment money put in when Nora's work was started for the secret lab. For five percent of the profits, he put up two hundred grand.

"He's damned sharp! He doesn't make bad investments, so I have to believe you when you say this is worth a billion."

"Tony! I have to call Tony! He can give me the information he's keeping. It could help. I forgot all about him!"

"Before you call him let's finish this project here. It won't take very long and we won't have the added distraction of trying to make something fit that doesn't belong.

"For instance, Wilder isn't one of the voices on that tape."

"He's not? I wonder who could ... maybe there's another iron in this fire that we don't know about. We could get burned easily enough."

"Yeah. I think we have to sort out this murder in another way altogether. Nothing fits if we try to tie all of it into one package. There's something to stop us at every new fact. Let's try looking at it as though each thing were a separate incident. It makes more sense that way.

"First, we had the murder of Gus Eisingstein. Consider that as one thing that's not connected to anything else. See what we have to work with there."

"He was killed in a sealed vault. The murderer got in by stowing away inside of a crate. He waited until Gus had finished some very important thing in his research to kill him, then went out the front door, taking those notes and that tape. He came back later to erase his leaving from the tapes. That was done, excluding anyone else for the obvious reasons, by either Nora or Ed. George couldn't have done it because he was used to deliver the crate. Ralph couldn't have done it because his size made it impossible for him to have delivered the fatal blow.

"Next, we have the death of.... No! Next we have those notes and the cassette copy left on Nora's front seat. That could go to motive or it could be because Nora wanted that research.

"Question: Why weren't we told about the two silent partners?

"Question: How – I just thought of this one – did our culprit know so much about the security arrangements here? About erasing the tapes? About the cameras not being focused on the end of that loading platform?

"Question: Motive?

"*Now* we have the second murder. Ralph...."

"Hold it!" Len said quickly. "I think maybe you left out the most important question of all about Gus Eisingstein.

"Question: Why was the murder weapon substituted?"

"Good lord! That's right! The blade found in the wound is *not* the one that *made* the wound! That could well mean Slats has our most important piece of evidence in the exact shape and size of the wound. There's every chance that murder weapon is distinct enough that it would point out the one and only person who could have used it."

"Uh-huh! It could also mean the weapon's one anyone here would recognize at once, so the killer wouldn't dare to leave it. I think that knife is important. I think there's a chance the case of Gus Eisingstein somehow hinges on the murder weapon."

"I see. It was distinctive enough that it could have some

kind of ritual significance? A wide, deep blade?

"Nothing in this case is going to surprise me."

Len picked up the phone, called Slats on his car unit and asked about the knife wound. The conversation was on the speaker.

"I have that in the report," Slats replied. "There are several things that don't make much sense, but that's the only thing that stands out to any great degree. I think it would be wise for you to concentrate on that knife, if just because there aren't many around and somebody might have seen it.

"The blade is at least eight and a half inches long, is three inches wide and is curved. Like one of those Egyptian things you see in the sheik movies."

Len talked a minute, then hung up.

"A fancy Egyptian dagger from the Arabian Nights!" he exploded. "Gus was a Jew, so we might have a terrorist killing!"

"Not bloody likely! The very last thing any terrorist would want is to hide the fact it's a terrorist attack. What would be the point? Besides which, Gus wasn't doing anything terrorists would get any points for knocking him off for. Just the fact he was a Jew doesn't make it a terrorist killing."

"Before you dismiss that part altogether you'd better remember that Ralph was a Jew, too," Len said, with a thoughtful look. "So far, that's the only thing we have that ties this mess together in any way.

"There's no reason to believe Ralph *wasn't* killed with the same knife, is there?"

He called Slats again to ask if it was provable whether Ralph was or was not killed with the same knife that Gus died from.

"The same knife? I don't see that.... I guess it's.... I'll call back in five minutes. The angle of overlap might show me something. I won't need a full lab for something so simple.

Give me a few minutes."

He left the line open, so I knew we had his curiosity aroused. Len and I both sipped the coffee and said nothing until Slats came back on the line.

"The end of the cut was slightly more upward than the start, so cut another path. The knife that killed Ralph Meiner was at least seven inches long and was curved. I can't say it was the same knife, but it was its twin, if not.

"Later!" He hung up.

"Curiouser and curiouser," Len quoted. "Are you *sure* it's not a terrorist thing?"

"It simply doesn't make any sense as a terrorist attack. They don't operate that way. It could be racist in some way, but that doesn't make much sense, either. I have a hard time thinking of it as a personal thing.

"Try this: Someone knocks Gus off because of the gene research thing. Greed.

"Everyone knows from the minute Slats announced it that the blade found in the wound wasn't the murder weapon. Ralph has seen someone with a ... that doesn't make much sense, either. Nobody's said anything about it being a strange Egyptian dagger, only that it wasn't the knife found in the wound because the wound was deeper and wider."

"I remember you saying the knife had some kind of knob on it because otherwise the killer would have a lump where he butted Gus. Maybe that's the giveaway, not the curved blade."

"That's reaching a bit, but it's not impossible. We've now tied the two murders together again. I thought the main object was to keep them separated. I don't think they can be separated. It's all one and the same thing. We have to find the other partner or partners and we have to find the people in those voiceprints. We know about when to look at the records at the lab, so maybe we can find them. Everyone who came and went is saved on tape."

"Unless our murderer decided to excise all of that stuff. I haven't spread it around about us finding the two background voices, so maybe he'll feel safe about that. Maybe he won't know we can enhance it. He'll definitely think we won't have any reason to look for anyone back then."

"I don't think our murderer is one of those voices. I think knowing who they are will lead to the real motive behind it, though. I think that whatever they were there for was what he was killed about. I think the killer played those tapes to be certain nothing was carried on them that would give us a clue, then put them in Nora's car so the research would be finished, either because of the money it will bring or because he believes in the work very strongly.

"We have to know who the other silent partner is and if there are any more than the two. I begin to wonder if Gus was killed because of one reason and Ralph because someone found he had sold, say, two or three hundred percent of the company? That's something we'll have to consider very very carefully."

"Someone would be screaming by now. It's not going to be that. Everyone knows Gus is dead and that he was working on a very important project. The fact it's already been on the news that Ralph is also dead would bring any investors right out. The fact our silent partner isn't hurrying to identify himself is a very suspicious circumstance."

"Maybe, and maybe not. There can be any number of other reasons for that – including that the killer's close enough to know everything's safe as it stands. I agree that having a number of investors would bring out some of them, but word will have to spread. Twenty four hours and we'll know.

"We have Gus and Ralph both killed with the same knife, so the two murders are related. We can't deny that. The fact we don't know the motive yet doesn't help at all.

"I'm calling Tony. Maybe he'll have answers instead of

more questions."

I used the phone and left it on speaker. There wasn't any reason to hide anything from Len.

"Tony? CD here. I've been running around all afternoon. There was another murder, so we can't play silly games anymore.

"What do you have?"

"CD! Thank god! I've been going crazy trying to run you down.

"You wanted to know about anyone who was trying to sell the gene process to some other country?

"Well, there *was* someone! He's been in contact with Israel for more than three months, minimum, so I can safely assume he was trying to sell the process to them. I can give you the names of the contacts."

"Ed Vore, right?" Len said smugly.

"Why, no. It was Gus, himself. Gus Eisingstein!"

Chapter four

That was a bit of an unexpected thing, but it was also logical, from one point of view. Gus would naturally be the one who might want to profit from the discovery – but it gave all the rest a motive to kill him. They could get cut out of their share.

Drop back ten yards and punt. I looked at the names Tony gave me. Len sat back in his creaky chair, looking expectant.

"I can see by the look on your face this didn't clear anything up for you, did it?"

"All it does is make me wonder what the hell Ralph saw or did to get himself killed,. Tony says Shartz and Auermond are both aliases for Israeli agents who work for the ... I guess you'd have to call it the World Agricultural Research Committee or something. I don't know how they figure in this. I don't know how any of this adds up.

"OK. George took the killer in. The killer knifed Gus, then left by the process we figured. The killer used a distinctive knife. That's what we have on the killing, itself. The killer waited for something to happen in that vault before killing Gus. There was something else that had to be finished before Gus was eliminated.

"That's assumed, but it's fairly certain. There simply isn't any reason I can see for the killer to wait that long.

"Now for pure supposition.

"Ralph knew that knife and Ralph knew who owned that knife. It had to be someone Ralph wouldn't believe would kill anyone, so he ... called the killer up and asked if he still had the knife. The killer acted confused and surprised he would be asked about it and took it over to Ralph's place to explain why he had.... Crap! Then why was all that information given to Nora? We have to know why any of this happened. It didn't have a single solitary damned thing to do with the money! I believe that less and less!"

"That's the only motive we have to work from. Take it away and none of it makes any sense.

"Gus was killed with some, as you call it, distinctive knife. If this was a ritualistic killing there would have been no reason to hide the fact. There wouldn't have been some laboratory tool substituted in there. The place wouldn't have been set up in some feeble attempt to make it look like a suicide. The same holds true about terrorism. The fact that both victims were Jews wouldn't hold that theory, anyhow.

"We don't have enough. That's the only thing that stays, no matter how many angles you try to look at it from. It's a lot like those trig problems with all kinds of information, but that don't have the one part you *need*!

"CD, I don't want to have to solve some damned psycho killings here! They bog the whole department down, waste time and wreck the budget. I just don't see what else we have!"

"I think it's legwork time. I have to find our missing link.

"Can we run everyone we come up with in this thing back a few generations? Even if it's a psycho there's some basic reason. I'll get Tony to do as much as he can. He'll have to find who the other silent partners are. I'm going to work on the Carson Wilder character – simply because I don't know what else to do."

"Cal will help trace whatever he can through his State Highway Patrol connections," Len answered. "I'll get Clarice to work with the computer stuff. She runs all our computers here, so maybe she can come up with something different. All I ask is one little thing to connect this up besides coincidence or the `Maybe he saw something' bit."

"Good luck!" I said, then stood, stretched, tossed down the last bit of coffee and left. I sat in the Trans Am for a few minutes trying to think of where to go. Nothing.

I went home and worked in the cattleya house, potting a weird cross Jim had made of Barkeria skinneri on Cattleya Obrieniana alba. It left my mind free, but I just couldn't find an angle.

"CD?" Tony answered when I called him early in the morning. "I found two other partners by tracing back through financial records and correspondence Ralph gave me when I was over there. There's a Yusef Kharavor, some kind of minor dignitary or something, and a Silvia Marks.

"Silvia Marks is in her late eighties and is in poor health. She lives in Sun City, up near Tampa.

"Carson Wilder lives on Anna Maria Island. You can find him easily enough. Early sixties, insurance broker. Seems to be clean enough. No record of anything.

"I can't find much of anything on Kharavor. He seems to live somewhere in the Gainesville area, but I can't find any listings. His letters are all from a P. O. box number there.

"I've made a disk of everything I could find and have it all listed, but there isn't very much there.

"I delivered the `bug chasers' to Ed Vore on my way in this morning and talked with Nora and George. Nora stayed there all night cloning the corn with the gene splice. George had just come in.

"Now! Are you ready for a shocker?"

"Anything to give me some kind of a break. What shocking news did you find?"

"The Israeli agents were seen at various times hanging around the labs. Nora saw them in the offices twice. George saw them in the hall by Ralph's office last week."

"That's very interesting, but it's *not* so shocking," I replied, with a questioning look. "So finish the news already."

"They aren't on those tapes. Anywhere."

"Not even in the halls?"

"Not anywhere, anyplace, any spot. Never. Not at any time."

"Is that possible? Are you saying George and Nora are lying?"

"I doubt it. Ed's foolproof security system, like all such things, ain't quite all it's cracked up to be. Those international spies have found a way to get around it."

"Tony, I don't want to get involved with spies!" I wailed in disgust. "That gets us bogged down in situations.... Oh, hell! How do they do it?"

"I can think of a way or two, but they'd first have to get access to the computers, somehow. Let's meet there in, say, two hours. I'll bring a friend from the plant who knows computers and who has some crazy ideas that seem to work. You have access to the sec room so we can maybe find something to hang this on."

"I'll be there," I said and hung up.

So. Things were starting to move. I hoped there wasn't a brick wall in the way to cause a sudden, painful stop.

Cliché time.

I parked next to the company car by the Dumpster and got out. Tony and some teenage kid got out of their car and came to meet me.

"This is John Kiley," Tony introduced. "He's good at computers and designs systems for us now and then. This is your boss, CD, JK – we call John JK. CD owns control of the Crane crap, as he calls it.

"We'll go through the system and you see what occurs to you about how to get through it without being on the sec records."

I reached to shake hands with JK, who suddenly wandered over to the lab door to look at the cardkey slot. He came back and grinned sheepishly at me and asked to see my cardkey. I handed it to him.

"Uh, nice to meet you Mr., uh, CD. I, uh, got an idea. I need the residual scan tracer, Tony."

He went to the car as Tony shrugged and grinned at me. "He's a genius. He'll seem sorta strange to you. Don't get upset when he suddenly takes off on some tangent and forgets you exist. He's like that.

"I wonder what he's doing."

JK took my cardkey, put it in a little shaped box he plugged into the car's lighter, attached a computer keyboard, watched the squiggles on the screen a minute, then typed a message on the qwerty board. Tony and I stood behind him to watch. He suddenly grinned, typed a message using control mode in a small spot on the screen and punched "copy." He took my card from the box, folded the screen and handed me the card.

"That's how they did it. Let's go in and see *when* they did it."

Tony shrugged and grinned and we went inside and to the sec room door.

"Here's where we find when they did it," JK said. "They had to make the one trip here to get the badge, so the cameras followed them that trip. They excised it, but the time sequence will be there."

We went through the door and directly into the sec room, where JK stood looking around for about two minutes. He went around to all the screens, then went to sit in front of the master. We waited about three more minutes. JK was lost in some other world. Tony shrugged again, and asked, "What now?"

"Oh, sorry," JK said. "Let's see how well it worked."

He snapped the tape out of the slot on the sec recorder and dropped another in after shifting the system to tape two. He dropped the tape into the playback/editor and ran it back for half an hour, then fast-forwarded it to a few minutes ago.

We were suddenly in the hall, coming toward the sec room. There was no record of the door being used. Tony grinned and shrugged again.

"Now, let me see the badges," JK ordered. "This system is so simple it ... I mean, didn't the guy who set this up know anything about feenth-code gobbledygookial fromishkyty biclopthdip parasystems at all?" (It sounded like that to me and apparently to Tony, too, who shrugged. He grinned and shrugged a lot around JK, as I was to learn over a period of time.)

He took the three badges, put them in the imprint slot and did something to them, then handed me mine and Tony his.

"Go on to the offices, then to the vault, use the key there, then come back here. You don't have to stop or spend any time. Just follow the route."

Tony grinned and shrugged and we went. We were back in about five minutes. JK snapped the tape from the recorders and dropped in a new one, then dropped it into the readout. We weren't on anything! It was like we never existed!

"Okay. You instructed the computers not to see us," Tony said. "How?"

"The sec system identifies everything and everyone through a digital input on the key. It follows you through the badges. Even the videocams are channeled through the comps, so I programed a nul code for you. You don't exist in the program so you aren't recorded. It's done all the time for TV and that sort of crap. Blue screen. You watch all those commercials where they do an overprint or overlay on a background. All you have to do is tell the machine not to put the overlay on. It's as simple as that. We can play back all the tapes on the com search for time gap sequences and find exactly when they started this. If we excise our little walk from the door to here from the tapes we cease to have ever been here, but the time gap is there to find unless I program it in as filler and do a nul sequence on the primary processor reconform fribbleedyfram gooflunk."

"If they did the excision and the badge program they thought of that," Tony said. "It isn't important when they started it, is it, CD?"

"I don't think so. This is what I wanted. It explains what our killer was waiting for, I think. Can you bring out what was there, but wasn't recorded on the tapes ... I guess not."

"It was never recorded," JK said. "Can't bring out what isn't there."

"We'll get back to the plant," Tony said. "Shartz and Auermond are staying at the Days Inn on forty one. I suppose you'll want to discuss a thing or two with them?"

It was my turn to grin. I could figure about what had happened now. Gus had a visitor or two, the killer simply waited for them to leave, then killed Gus. It was going to be rough to get those two agents to admit to anything whatever, but I had a lever: I knew how they did it and could pull off a bit of a bluff of my own – unless they were the ones who killed Gus. If that were so I was back to nothing at all making sense instead of only ninety eight percent not making sense. If they killed Gus the one I thought was the killer, the one who blanked the tapes when he left, was a witness to the killing and.... No way! Ralph wouldn't be dead, in that case!

I went to the Days Inn, found the rooms Tony told me the two were staying in and went up to knock. I was in luck. Auermond was there. I introduced myself, he introduced himself and I asked if I could speak to him about the lab and what they wanted there.

"Lab? I'm afraid I have no vague idea what you're talking about," Auermond replied smoothly. "I haven't been to any labs of any kind. I'm merely on a vacation with a friend, doing some fishing and seeing the sights, such as they are."

"There's a backup – or was a few days ago – on the comps. Your badges and keycards only blank out the main system cams. The secondary records everything at all times on straight video. Before you tell me about the debugging devices, the backup is in Vore's private office in a filing cabinet. The debuggers won't detect anything because the scan cameras are always on, so I'd greatly appreciate it if we drop the bullshit routines. I'm not in the least interested in your spy bit. I'm trying to solve a murder."

"Four months of fishing would get a bit tiresome I'd think."

I got a look of pure cold steel, so I grinned at him. He stood aside and I went in.

"I'm somewhat puzzled by all this. What do you want and what do we have to do with it?"

"The killer was hiding in the secure vault when you talked with Gus Eisingstein. There's a good chance that something you said or agreed on resulted in his death. I want to catch the killer, so I have to know what was said to determine who killed him and why."

"For the record, I have no least conception of what you're talking about. Off the record, I want to know who did it, myself. It will very probably be the same person who killed Meiner. I don't want to have anyone who kills an Israeli get away with it!

"Eisingstein discovered a process – you know about that – that would feed Israel and would allow us to feed a hell of a lot of other hungry people. He discussed giving the process to Israel. We were financing his research since he had the original idea, but the others at the labs wouldn't see it as ours or his because he was a partner in the thing. He was to bring his research and the embryos and become an Israeli citizen next Friday. We arranged for his flight out at our meeting. We left the lab at about two o'clock. No one else was around.

"That's all I'll have to say about it. You can draw your own conclusions."

"Me? Fine. I conclude that Eisingstein was an American citizen, as was Ralph. They were *not* Israeli citizens. I conclude you are engaged in espionage against this country. I conclude that the genetic research was stolen from Nora Seely and I conclude you perfectly well knew it. I further conclude Gus was being paid by, was using the facilities of and had various contractual agreements with the labs and that any financing you did was minor and irrelevant.

"My personal feelings are that the process should be worldwide and in the public domain so Israel or anywhere else can't hold those they might perceive to be their enemies under threat of starvation or under economic thralldom due simply to the fact you control a process and would use it as a weapon.

"I know very well your type are a minority in Israel if a powerful one.

"I lastly conclude you are scum of the worst kind.

"You can come to your own conclusions as to whether it would be wise for you and your fellow foreign espionage agent to be out of this country within twelve hours and never to return. My name is Carlisle Devon Grimes. You can check on me and my connections with the Crane companies, but do it fast. I may be a minority here in the US, but I'm a damned powerful one, in myself. I think you can pretty quickly determine exactly how much value you and your friend will have as agents in the future when you determine how much I have to spend on fingering you wherever you go.

"Goodbye. Have a pleasant day."

Well, he *was* a foreign agent – and he *did* corrupt an American citizen. He *was* attempting to steal technology and I didn't doubt for one second his little group planned to use the process as a weapon. There are plenty of the same type running things in this country – and I don't mean Jewish citizens. Race or religion has nothing to do with it.

I shouldn't allow my temper to get away with me like that, but facts are facts. The killer heard Gus make an agreement to skip out on his obligations and contracts. Those people were operating illegally in this country. Those people had also corrupted Gus for political gain to be derived from an important new biological process actually discovered by Nora Seely. I have no doubt whatever they would try to keep the process secret and under their sole control, at all costs. I'm equally sure Gus thought he was doing a great service for his own people.

That's the saddest part of it. He was intending to willingly become a traitor to the US because of a line of unadulterated horse manure fed to him in the guise of humanitarian action. If those people were actually so gung-ho for feeding the starving masses of the world they would've been financing the research amid great publicity, telling the third world to begin preparing areas that could be irrigated with salt water because they would shortly be getting seed.

OK. Off the soapbox. Certain aspects of the case were beginning to fit into their places. I had to find the connection now to someone who reacted in a violent fury because Gus was going to give the process to Israel. I could see several possibilities, such as: The profit would be lost to the company altogether for a process developed under contract, thus each partner would lose his tailfeathers.

Someone was too much an idealist and didn't want the process held over the third world as an economic weapon.

Someone didn't want *Israel* to have the process. Period!

There were a few other possibilities, but those seemed most likely.

I remembered something about when we met in Ralph's office. George Seely and Ralph Meiner were both rather vehemently opposed to Israel getting the process and they both said Gus would take it straight to them. Gus was dead and Ralph was dead – but, damnit – George couldn't have done it! Period! George took the killer into that vault! Nothing else would work. Had someone *else* tampered with the badges and keys?

No. They were all on the tapes all along. They couldn't change the badges and cardkeys back and forth. They didn't have the equipment Crane and the foreign agents had.

I'd have to check Carson Wilder, Silvia Marks and that Yusef character. Silvia was least likely, so she would wait. Wilder was close, so I'd drop in on him first.

I drove out to Anna Maria and along until I found the address Tony had given me. There were electronically locked gates, so I drove up and talked into the phone on a box beside the gate to a butler or something. It took a few minutes, but the gates finally slid back and I drove in. As I drove along the winding tar drive it hit me I hadn't done anything yet about getting those two Israeli agents out of the country, so I used the phone in the Trans Am to call Tony to explain what I'd said and done. He said it would be handled and Crane would keep tabs on the two. He really *would* see they were fingered anywhere they went.

Carson Wilder was much as described. He was something of a stuffed shirt, but was trying to be oh-so magnaminious to my type of lesser quality trash, like those phony pseudo-liberals in the sixties and seventies. His condescending attitude was about to get to me when we went around to the "back lawn," where he had a small neat greenhouse. I could see some top quality orchids blooming inside the door and there was a plant of Pot. Screaming Feather "Redgold" FCC/AOS on a white wrought iron and glass table outside.

"I see you have rather good taste in orchids," I said, hiding my glee. "That Screaming Feather was a good cross."

"Oh? You know orchids?" he said, his look saying very plainly there was no way I could afford a lousy backbulb from that plant.

"I have a few at my place in Englewood and some in the Bonita Springs hideaway. The stuff Grams and Greatgramps did is mostly in the Nicely range, but I have a lot of the better studs – like the Screaming Feather and Sheila's Dream and so forth – here."

"Er, you have, er, studs of the Crane and Grimes plants – oh! I see! You *are* a Grimes! Relatives?" he asked, with a bit of a sneer.

"Well, JR, who made the cross, was Great-gramps and Sheila Grimes was Grams. I have all their stuff now. Only brat in the line who cares about them in such a strong way, you know.

"What I have to know about this stuff is if you had any idea of what Gus was working on."

"But...! The Crane companies? I thought the one with the orchids was.... I mean.... I didn't know the detective was.... The orchid society said CD.... Oh! You *are* C. D. Grimes? You *own* Crane?!"

"Only fifty one percent. Really. This murder is more important than any of that stuff."

"But you ... but ... but, I own some Crane stock! You must be worth hundreds of millions!"

"Well, actually, it's something over eight billion, at the present moment. Really. That's not important. This murder is."

"I don't have any idea what anyone's doing there," he replied, staring at me strangely. "I invested a bit when Nora Seely told me about the place. She makes up the flasking solutions for the local orchid society, though she doesn't grow the plants. It's all stuff they use in culture plates or something. It was mostly a tax shelter that could turn into a very profitable thing or could go wholly bust. I don't know anything except that I get five percent of any profits."

"You would have no objections if Gus were to have given the rights to the process they developed to Israel?"

"I don't care a hoot one way or the oth – *given*?!" he yelled. "Damned right I object! Nobody told me anything about *giving* anything away! The place is there to make a profit! I don't give a damn in hell if they sold it to Israel or Red China or Russia, but they damned well better not be *giving* anything away! I'll sue their asses off! What are you talking about?!"

"Oh, Gus was knocked off before he was able to follow through with the plan. He did have that in mind, though.

"Pray tell me, Mr. Wilder. Would you kill someone to prevent them giving a process away?"

"You get the hell out of here! I don't give a damn who you are or what you've got! I don't like the way you make implications at all! That's outrageous!

"For your information, if they give anything – anything – away I can collect my full percentage of its market value. That's in the contract and solely at my option. I resent your intimation that I'd ever kill anyone over something like that! It's not that much! One process wouldn't be worth that much! I resent that! Get the hell off of my property! Stay off!"

"The process is worth a flat billion," I said, heading for my car. "Your five percent would be fifty million. That sounds like a fair motive to me.

"Bye!"

"Wait! Are you serious? They owe me fifty million dollars?"

"Nope! They don't owe you a single plugged penny. Gus was knocked off before he gave the thing away. Nothing's been done with it, as a result."

"They *have* a process that's worth that, though?"

"If they can make it work it should be worth a good part of

that. Maybe the killer cooled Gus a little too soon and they won't be able to figure it out to a point where they can sell it. You'll have to wait to see what they're able to do with it. Them's the breaks.

"Bye!"

I drove out with him staring blankly at the spot I'd left. The gate opened automatically if anyone wanted out.

OK. George didn't do it and Carson Wilder didn't do it. Silvia Marks rather obviously couldn't have done it. It was done by a person who knew those labs, knew the security system and knew the routine everyone, including Gus, followed. I would have to fly up to Gainesville to find Yusef Kharavor, but I stopped by Len's place first to catch him up to date on what I had. Cal saw me turning off the interstate and followed me into Englewood. We went on to the Harde Luck Cafe to discuss it and Leelah Harde, the owner, joined us. She likes to keep up with what we're doing. I explained everything and what I thought now. Maybe George and Wilder were out as suspects, but no one else was.

"I think it was your two spies," Leelah said.

"No. They left before Gus was killed. He was killed because of his discussion with them. We have that excision on the tapes. Someone else was there."

"You *said* they know everything about those computers! They could go in there and erase a few minutes so you'd *think* someone else was there."

"I hate to say it, but you could be right," Cal said. "Gus was killed because of his discussion with the spies, but it could be because he told them to stick it. Maybe he was going to hold out on them or expose them or something."

"Oh, groan!" Len cried. "We don't need this! Tony called not half an hour ago and said they were already heading out of the country!"

"They didn't do it. As much as I wish it was something like

that, they couldn't have done it. They would've taken the notes. Nora wouldn't have them now. They would still have the process – and would already be gone."

"Don't you watch television?" Leelah asked. "They have little spy cameras for that. Crane *makes* the damned things! They photograph all the material or copy all the tapes, then give the originals back to throw you off their trail. They would still have the stuff."

"It wouldn't have the value they're looking for, that way," Len said. "The third world and the Arabs would still end up with the process because Nora Seely will go ahead and finish it.

"I've got twenty four hour guards on Nora. I want to be very damned sure that process *is* completed!"

"So does the killer. That's why she has the stuff.

"What we're down to is someone doesn't want *Israel* to have the process, but they do want everyone else to have it. It's someone who's familiar with the labs. They knew about the sec system, the habits of the people there and Ralph knew them well enough that he was killed because of something that occurred to him."

"Then it was Nora, George or that Ed Vore character," Len said. "George is out. We don't have anything else!"

"Or Wilder is a good actor or that second partner, Silvia What's-her-face, isn't nearly as old or sick as reported or one of them hired – oh, shit!" Cal said. "Someone could have hired it done. A professional hit man would get all the information about the rest of it."

"It was someone who had enough access to figure what Gus was doing. That still leaves the same ones. Someone at the labs or a partner. It would be a partner, regardless. Yusef Kharavor is in Gainesville, so I'll call on him this afternoon. I want to know if he's like Ralph – a Jew who thinks this kind of thing should be kept out of Israeli hands, at all costs."

"Jewish?" Len asked. "Is he Jewish? The name sounds more like Russian or something to me – and the Ruskies would just photograph the evidence and steal it.

"Uh-oh!"

"Yeah!" Leelah said. "They might even give the notes and tapes back, mightn't they?"

"The name's from one of those places like Afganistan, I'd say," Cal said. "That way they'd do anything to keep it *away* from Russia."

All at once I was very much interested in meeting this Yusef Kharavor character!

Chapter five

Gainesville and the area are spread out enough to where it wasn't going to be an easy job to find someone from just a name and P. O. box number. I tied down the Cessna and rented a car, then went to the post office at the proper zip code. I found the box number, then went to the information window. I didn't expect any information and I didn't get any.

Next stop was the obvious. I stopped at a phone booth to look in the directory, but there wasn't anything under any Kharavor that was at all promising. I called everything that even might be connected, but there was no Yusef or Joe among the group. That left me the one thing I hate about the detective business.

There had been a couple of letters and a small package in the box visible behind the glass, so I perched on a bench to wait for someone to pick the stuff up. When no one came by seven I got a meal and checked into a nearby motel, called Len, called Tony and called home. There wasn't much new there, so I read a book and went to bed.

It was seven ten in the morning and I had been sitting on that bench for forty minutes when a darkhaired girl came to open the box and take the mail out. I decided to follow her because *she* obviously wasn't Yusef Kharavor and I wanted something to do. If I were to approach her to ask about him it could get sticky if she had orders to not lead anyone to him. I don't know why I felt he was trying to avoid me or anyone with business with the labs. He probably didn't have any idea I existed and surely wouldn't know anyone was more than peripherally interested in him. He most likely didn't know anyone knew he was a partner in the place.

The girl got into a little Hyundai and drove about half a

mile into a zoned area where there were a bunch of small industrial businesses and warehouses. I stayed a block back or more, but her car was easy to find when she pulled off the access road into a parking lot by a blocky warehouse. There was a sign in front and another beside the door. Far East Exotic Imports. Wholesale and retail. The girl opened a padlock on a hasp, then rolled the accordion steel shutters up from in front of the large plate glass window in front. There were baskets, tapestries and an assortment of trinkets in the window. She then removed a huge padlock from a hasp to roll the steel shutter up in front of the door, then used two keys on the door itself. She went in, putting an **Open for Business** sign on the door.

I went along the access road until I found a small cafÉ and went in for coffee and a heated Danish. The waitress didn't know anything about the businesses over in "that section" because they all went to the Armenian restaurant over on Redwood Street.

Redwood was about eight blocks back the way I came. I rushed to finish the coffee and went back. The little restaurant was neat and clean and was set back from the street enough for a double row of cars and panel trucks out front. I found a space, parked and went to the door where an interesting little sign said

WELCOME!

Please leave where you or your ancestors came from outside

I liked the place already!

There were long wooden tables haphazardly arranged around the floor. It seemed people just dragged the tables and chairs around to suit them and it suited them to have ten or twelve to a table. There were several tables in little alcoves to one side.

The long tables had Orientals, blacks, whites – from very dark to very blond – and various mixtures sitting around discussing taxes and sales, joking and, on one long table, playing dominoes. The tables in the alcoves seemed to all be very dark people or Oriental people at individual tables. Those were the ones the sign on the door was directed at. Little cliques who stayed with their own kind.

A dark pretty girl came to ask what I wanted.

"Arabian coffee and a pecan Danish, heated. Where do I sit?"

"You're new. Anywhere you can find a seat. There aren't any individual tables left. Everybody plops down where they can. If you don't play dominoes you really shouldn't sit there. I'll find you."

She rushed off to the kitchen. I sat at a table where there was a space by simply grabbing an empty chair and pulling it to the spot. The Japanese fellow on one side said, "Hi! I'm Niko."

"CD. Nice little place."

"It's convenient. We all come here before work."

The black on the other side introduced himself as Mark. We chatted about aluminum-frame windows (Niko) and electrical contracting (Mark) for a few minutes. I talked about office electronics and security systems because Crane makes all that stuff and I'm not a complete dummy around the subject. About ten 'til eight they both said they had to get to work, so I asked about the import place down the road.

"Those people are all at table three," Niko said. "They feel too elite to mingle with us peons. They only have their special friends to ever come in here. The one over there seems to be the boss. Some of the ones he meets give me the creeps!"

"I think it's maybe because they don't speak very good English," Mark suggested. "'Course, they don't *want* to speak much English if it means they got to mix with us trash. I know just what Niko means about the creepy ones. They're a bunch of mob types, if you ask me! All the big secrets! Way they act makes you want to fucking puke!

"Sorry. We don't talk that way in here. I'm out of line. If they want to meet with a bunch of hoods that's their business.

"Nice to meet you, CD! Hope to see you soon!"

Table three, if I was right about which one it was, had four dark men sitting around it who almost studiously ignored everyone else in the place. I memorized them, then went to the door, paid the check and left.

I sat across from Far East Exotic Imports for more than an hour before a big black Lincoln Town Car with those dark-filmed windows parked on the side of the building and two of the men from the restaurant got out and went in a side door. I gave them ten minutes, then drove into the place and parked next to the Hyundai. I strolled inside and asked the girl if Yusef Kharavor was in. She pulled a strap hanging behind her and one of the dark men from the restaurant came to ask what I required. There wasn't a thing wrong with his English.

"My name is CD Grimes. I wish to speak with you concerning the murders of two of your partners at the biolabs in Sarasota?"

He didn't bat an eye. He simply stepped back and made a wide sweeping gesture for me to enter the room he came from. "I think I saw you in the restaurant a few minutes ago?" I said, as I went past him.

"Yes. I meet others in the same kind of business there," he replied, offering me a seat. "The import business is a some-what exclusive one. We must ascertain among ourselves that we do not all bring in the same items or we may soon find ourselves without profitable markets. We meet with our overseas suppliers there at times to make trading agreements where we do not infringe on one another's territory.

"How is your investigation into the most unfortunate

deaths of Mr. Gustav Eisingstein and Mr. Ralph Meiner coming, Mr. Grimes? Have you yet been able to determine why this thing was done?"

So he knew about the whole mess and knew all about me.

"In one sense, yes," I replied, making it a point not to bat an eye. Two can share that scene! "Eisingstein was going to give Nora's insert process to Israel, is the direct motive. Meiner saw something or was able to add something up, so he had to be killed to prevent his disclosing what he knew."

"And you feel the Israeli agents are not the culprits in all this?"

Again I didn't react. I think that was puzzling to him. He thought the first would get a reaction. When it didn't, he added the second even bigger bombshell – and I acted as though I would naturally expect him to know. It was easy enough to see he was very used to pulling strings and making others dance to whatever tune he was playing. He was *not* used to anyone who seemed to be a step ahead of him.

"Not the killers, no. The fact they were there and Eisingstein said the things he said to them may have resulted in the murders occurring so immediately, but they didn't kill Gus, so, logically, they didn't kill Ralph."

"That is a relief to know. Their having left the country last evening would place you in a very difficult spot, should they be guilty of these things.

"One may travel the world, and I predict you will before this is over, to find all the bits and pieces of the entire puzzle. I think you should never forget that it would take the wiles of Cleopatra and the wisdom of Solomon to hold a thing so large as this together for any length of time. It is possibly going to be much older, larger and more sinister than you could guess.

"How may I assist you in any of this? I was here, so can only report on my poor secondhand information." He was watching me carefully now, though everything except his eyes was seemingly unconcerned and uninterested. I dropped another of my own little bombshells to see if *he* would react. "I feel that, as you have such excellent information about what is happening at those facilities, you may perhaps have been informed of something I haven't been able to dig up yet. You must admit to the fact that your own intelligence is quite good. Perhaps something was reported in the past couple of months that would help to resolve it."

"No, I'm afraid not. I didn't excessively concern myself with the place until very recently, when it became quite clear Mr. Esingstein was stealing Mrs. Seely's research. I tend to watch my own investments quite closely, Mr. Grimes. Mr. Eisingstein's political bent is well known to me, as it also is to certain others. It was most obvious he would tend to give anything with such a great potential to impact on the situation in the East to Israel. Very frankly, that would result in a great loss – of funds – to me. I wished only to ensure that such an event would never transpire."

The way he was watching me it was obvious he expected me to say something like, "How far did you go to ensure that?" – so I merely nodded. That pause about "funds" meant a lot. A *whole* lot, I thought!

About what? I had a long way to go here.

I let the silence grow for a moment, then stood. "Thank you. You've been *very* helpful," I said, offering my hand and a smile.

I won whatever that contest was about. I got a reaction: "That's *all*?!"

I wanted to know more than anything in the world exactly how he got his information. He fully expected me to ask and he would then tell me. I would be guided from that point to exactly where he wanted me to go. It wouldn't be that hard to discover his source for myself and he would worry and wonder about how much I knew all along and how much of it he didn't know. I smiled again and left.

OK. We played a little game and I won – but where, exactly, was I? *What* had I won?

He had a quick and complete contact with the research lab. It would have to be one of the people working there or one of his partners. It was definitely not Nora. His statement that her research was being pirated, the phrasing, left no doubt of that, and it wasn't Sylvia Marks because she wasn't in any position to know anything. It probably wasn't Carson Wilder because I didn't think he knew what the hell was going on anywhere.

George Seely might be reporting directly to him because he wanted to protect Nora's work. Ed Vore might be reporting to him because ... of something?

If there was anyone there I didn't know much about in this it was definitely George, but that didn't mean he had anything to do with the murders. He didn't.

What if the Israeli agents reported to Kharavor? What if he was their clearinghouse?

I picked up a couple brochures on my way out, smiled at the pretty salesgirl and headed back to the little Armenian restaurant. I wanted to know where Kharavor was from. I felt it would clear up a lot of this.

There were almost no customers in the place, now that the local businesses were open, so I asked the table girl about Yusef Kharavor.

"Didn't you see the sign on the door? It means just what it says!"

"I'm investigating a muh ... uh, scam. It's very possible he's involved, either as a victim or as a progenitor (I like that word!)."

"Oh, just about everyone knows he's been smuggling stuff in. That whole bunch are, but it's piddling little stuff. We know there aren't any drugs or that sort of things, but there may be jewels and art. That the sort of thing you mean?"

"Only in small part. I'm not directly investigating him. I'd know everything about him if I was. It's something that came up about someone else that may connect him is all. I want to save as much time as I can. If he's from Afganistan he's out of it on this end, though stuff can come through the Khyber Pass and ... but that's not what it's about."

"Houlmunn, the one who always sits with his back to the rear wall, is Afgan," she said. "Muhim, the one who sat across from Kharavor, is Egyptian. Hamout is Indian. Kharavor is mixed, but his mother was Iranian and his father was from Lebanon, though he was supposed to be either Palestinian or Jordanian. I don't know for sure. That's stuff that I heard from others. They've all been coming here since we opened three years ago. They stay to themselves."

I gave her a big tip and thanked her, then went to the car to head for the airport.

Hoo boy! If Kharavor was Palestinian or Jordanian, there was more motive than anyone could ask for to kill Gus Eisingstein to prevent his giving the process to Israel! That would mean his contact at the labs was the murderer. He could definitely prove beyond a doubt he was there in Gainesville when both murders took place. That could be counted on.

He *was* there, even if he'd ordered the killings directly. Now I was out of suspects again! George did *not* commit the murders! That left Ed Vore. Period.

There had to be a connection between Vore and Kharavor.

I thought Vore wouldn't be able to do it, but there were added factors, now. He would have been able to wait if those agents were in there. He was in the best position to report back to Kharavor. He could handle all the security stuff. He knew the research labs intimately. He knew everyone's established routines. He could use computers to find pretty much what everyone was doing at any given time by tracing the supplies they were using. He ran the inventory and ordering of all chemicals, supplies, tools and the rest of it.

I was suddenly surprised at myself. I'd told Auermond there was a separate surveillance system that recorded directly from the cameras instead of through a computer readout – and I *had* to have been right! Vore knew about those agents and knew what they were doing there!

I couldn't prove one little thing and knew it. I knew with moral certainty that Ed Vore was the killer, but I couldn't make any charge whatever because I didn't have a single fact to take to court that wouldn't be laughed out of the place.

Most of my cases are solved very quickly. I take the proof to court and they act on it. I don't bother to write about most of them except as reports in a file cabinet. I can forget about most of them, but this was different. This one was solved except for finding some kind of proof, but I knew certainly it wasn't yet half done. That proof was going to be hard to come by, but I was bound and determined to keep a promise I made when I first moved to Florida that no such murderer was going to get away with it in that place. I was going to hang this on Vore's neck by finding the proof and drawing the noose I made with that proof tighter and tighter until he was tied to Kharavor so tightly he would never be able to extricate himself.

My! Aren't I dramatic today!

I called Tony to tell him I wanted to have JK ready to spend whatever time necessary on those sec computers at the labs. I knew what we had to find and we would stay on it until it *was* found. I would also want some special equipment delivered to the labs. Tony would have it ready when I got back. I still had the cardkey that would leave me and guests off the computers. Maybe we could handle the bulk of this tonight and Vore would never be able to discover how we beat his system.

Maybe I'd enjoy this, after all!

I used the cardkey to let Tony, JK and myself into the labs. Nora's car was outside, so she would be in the roof lab working on the stuff from the notes and tapes Gus left there. She would probably stay locked in there all night. She wouldn't stop until she had what she was after anymore than I would. That suited me.

I explained to JK what I thought probably had happened. He said he'd find it if there was anything there.

Tony and I took a debugger and an induction meter around the hall. Sure enough, all the cameras had signal leads going into Ed's office.

"How do we get in there?" Tony asked. "They each have their own special cardkey to their own offices and a code on top of it."

"The code to his office is his birthdate. We have to find what it is and we have to find something we can use for a cardkey. JK should be able to do something for us there."

We went back to the sec room, where JK had four tapes already laying on the desk. He said he had a part of what we were looking for. I told him we needed something to use to get into Ed's office.

"Oh, that's no problem. He built one hell of a good security system here. It would be hard as hell to get around it without a lot of modern equipment, but he also did something that makes it almost worthless on the office and records room doors. I'll show you."

We went to the door to Ed's office, where JK asked Tony for the inductor. He slid the cardkey to Ralph's office, which I had left with him, into the slot and read the meter, then did it again, grinned, took a screwdriver from his belt and pried the facing strip to the door frame off. He reached in with the screwdriver, drew out some fine wires, put the induction meter on each wire as he ran the card into the slot and took two of them out. He cut into the insulation on the wires and jumped the one-ten line to one of the wires, then to the other. There was a click. He pushed the door open, wrapped some tape on the wires he'd bared, shoved all the wires back and tapped the facing strip back in place. There was no sign anything had been done there.

"Unless he pulls the wires out he can't tell anything was done in there, so don't move anything," he cautioned and went back to the sec room. Tony grinned and shrugged.

"I can figure that one myself. Read all the input and output lines with the card in place. The two that don't show anything operate the door. The weakness in the system is that the system's lines weren't cast into the wall or put in steel conduit or something."

"The system was put in here after the building was built and he used what was already there. Let's see what we can see."

There were eight VCRs in a cabinet with leads from the cameras going directly in. They would record for twelve hours or more. All of them were running.

Tony took each tape out, snapped it into the one on the set, rewound and ran it at fast forward. They were about three hours each, so we ran them all in less than half an hour. Nothing was on them except Nora and George coming in, Nora going to the roof lab, George dumping the trash and getting some files from his office and George leaving. Next was us coming in.

Tony erased all the tapes forty one minutes from start to the end of the recordings, then put them back in the VCRs, but pulled the plugs on the machines first so they would deprogram and stop recording.

"We'll find the indicator circuit," Tony said. "We can run the recorder back on it and show a line flicker. The sec room and labs are all on secondary surge protector safety circuits, but the offices aren't. He'll never be really sure. We can time the flicker for the forty one minutes. I'm sure he turns it all off when he's here."

I looked at all the red digital twelve o'clock numbers now flashing on the sets and grinned.

We searched the office and found a stack of VCR tapes, all labeled, in a locked desk drawer. Tony used a lockpick (*I'm the detective! I don't even know how to use a pick!*) to open all the locked drawers. We took all the tapes and went to the sec room.

JK said he had about everything there, but some of it wasn't in the computers. "I'd say it's all in a file somewhere. It would probably be in the administrator's office."

We searched Ralph's office thoroughly. There was a file cabinet marked "Personnel" – but it was empty. "I can get it back at the plant," JK said. "It's all public record. All I have to know is like a social security number, a driver's license number or anything like that."

"Damnit, JK! We don't *have* anything like that!" Tony protested as we headed out. "If we did we wouldn't have spent the time in Ralph's office looking for it!"

"But you've seen all their cars," JK said patiently. "What were the license plate numbers?"

"That's right! Driver's license number is on the license plate registration," Tony said. "Len will have that."

"I also have Kharavor's license number. You can trace that stuff from anywhere in the state, can't you?"

"I can trace it from anywhere in the solar system," JK said, then grinned and got a blank look. He wandered out toward the cars. Tony grinned and shrugged.

I was in the cool house, looking at a new Cypripedium Tommie Hanes cross, the first I had brought to flower since moving to Florida. It was going to be one spectacular cross!

"Honey! Plug in the phone in there! It's Tony," Alma called over the intercom.

I plugged in the phone and answered.

"CD? Are you sitting down?"

"I can handle it. Who's been murdered now?"

"You told me you wanted a direct connection between Kharavor and Ed Vore, right?"

"Definitely. That gives me enough motive to bring the rest of it up in court."

"How about the fact that Yusef Kharavor is the uncle of one Eduard Vore – nee Kharavor?"

"No shit!? That puts the noose right around both of their throats!"

"You won't be able to tag Kharavor. Ed had the same motive. You can't show that Kharavor had anything to do with it."

"Hell! He knew every detail of everything about that place! He damned well...! OK. You're right. I know it and you know it, but we aren't going to be able to prove any of it – yet.

"I'll handle friend Ed Vore. He did the actual murders, but Yusef pulled the strings. We'll tie Vore up and try to get the chair for him, then I'll find out what to do about Yusef."

"CD, I don't think we should try for the chair on this one. I don't sympathize with murder, but the way those people are being treated over there by the Israelis can make me understand it. If we were in Ed Vore's position and there was a Gus Eisingstein about to give them a bigger whip I'd do the same. So would you."

"Maybe, but I wouldn't kill Ralph and neither would you. It was between Gus, Yusef, Ed and those two agents. You or I either one would kill the bastard and take the breaks, if we got caught.

"OK. Murder one for Ralph, but not capital. I don't care if they drop charges for Gus. He *was* acting as a traitor. He *was* going to give important information to foreign agents."

"I'll go along with that. In case you want to know the real strength of their motive, Vore's grandparents – Kharavor's parents – had their homes bulldozed about six months ago by the Israelis. They were in their late seventies. They were accused of harboring terrorists, which was plainly ridiculous as the place was hardly more than a shack. There wasn't room for hiding anyone. The father is now in jail for not paying taxes to the Israeli government to pay for those soldiers now occupying the territory.

"CD, I didn't have any idea what was really going on there until we got into this! South Africa *and* the Nazis could take lessons!"

"You can't compare this to the Nazis. I figured it was pretty bad, though. Our lovely government wouldn't let us know too much about it because Israel is a so-called friendly government. I won't wonder why our `friends' have become the very things they were being protected from, why our 'friends' have spies working in this country or why so many of our so-called `friends' are major violators of our professed human rights restrictions."

"Your point about the Nazis is easy to answer!" It was the first time I ever heard him so close to telling me off. "It's all a matter of numbers, isn't it? You're willing to overlook atrocities if the numbers are low. The Nazis did it to thousands and the Israelis only do it to hundreds, so it's all right. That it?"

"Point taken. You're right. It's the same thing. Israel has become like Nazi Germany in a good number of ways, but we're not talking about thousands. In Germany it was millions."

"If it's only one it's still an atrocity! All this stuff, except the parts about the Kharavor family, is from Ralph Meiner's own personal notes. He was a Jew, but he adamantly hated those Israelis who keep this sort of thing going ... Ah! Here it is! This is a quote from a paper he wrote: `I've done the research, and find many of the figures don't hold up. There were a total of four million seven hundred thirty eight thousand Jews in those areas where the Nazis supposedly slaughtered six million. Not all of those less than five million were killed, as we all know. Hundreds of them are today alive and testifying at the trials. The same manner of atrocities were committed against Christians by the Muslims in the Balkans, possibly in greater numbers.

"`I cannot, and do not, condone this falsification of history, and I do not in any wise support the oppression of any people.

"`One would think the Jewish people would have learned their lesson about human reactions and about how low it is possible for a race to sink from the Nazis who, after all, DID much of what they are accused of.

"`Oh, Israel! I cry for the destruction you are bringing upon your own people! I cry for the fact that I will have to bear yet another burden. I cry for the lost chances of my people to ever become great.

"`Throughout all of history, no country that did these things is remembered except with loathing. All people of those races are forever cursed by such a history.'

"It goes on, but that's the vein. CD, Ralph would've probably helped the murderer! He was their friend!"

"So, are you saying we should let the person who killed his friend go?"

"No! I don't think we should be too punitive, either. I think he has to live with that. I think he realizes by this time he's become what he's fighting. Just like Israel."

"I think he was probably propagandized into it just like Gus was. I think Shartz and Auermond are guilty as hell of making Gus into a traitor and I think Kharavor is as guilty as hell of making a killer out of Vore. I think I made a hell of a mistake when I had you run those two out of the country. I think I'm going to see Kharavor doesn't get away with this, either. If it had just been Ed killing Gus maybe I'd be less ... I don't know.

"It's something that was sleazy and dirty from the beginning. It just got sleazier and dirtier. When Shartz and Auermond and Kharavor get away with sort of thing it gets steadily worse.

"I'm going to the lab to tag Vore. I'll call Len to meet me there. I want you to find everything there is to know about Yusef Kharavor. I want to know when he last farted and who curled their noses as a result. Everything."

"You got it."

We talked a minute more while I cooled off, then I called Len to meet me at the lab and told Alma I wouldn't be home for lunch. She rolled her eyes and grinned. Things were normal.

"I guess I knew you'd figure it out," Ed said half an hour later. "I could deny everything and you'd never get any proof. I don't believe you could make it stick, but I don't think, under the circumstances, a court will be too hard on me, either."

"If you'd stopped with Gus, I might agree. When you killed Ralph you sold your chances down the river. Ralph wasn't doing anything. He was actually on your side!"

"Hey! You wait just a fucking goddamned minute!" Vore shouted. "I didn't have a damned thing to do with killing Ralph! I swear! I don't know anything about that! Ralph wouldn't have done anything to hurt me! He *knew* all about my folks!"

I started a sharp retort, but for some reason I believed him. Killing Ralph never made any sense. I could see by the way Len was looking at me he felt the same.

"Then who *did* kill him? It was done with the same knife

you used on Gus!"

"That's something I couldn't tell you when I saw the knife was gone. It would have been admitting I killed Gus. I left the knife there! It was a sort of thing that would say it was a Palestinian who did it. I'd wiped it clean of prints. I was going to say the sec system was broached so it would look like some outside thing.

"I'll tell you what happened. Maybe you can make some sense of it. I know I can't!"

Chapter six

"It really started in several places at several times," Ed began. "It's hard to separate the things.

"My grandparents, my greatuncles and aunts, most of my cousins – all of them live in squalor and in constant fear and rage. They were just normal people trying to grub a living out of very hostile soil when it started. It would take days to tell of all the indignities and wrongs heaped on them by the occupying tyrants."

"We know about some of it," I interrupted. "We know about the bulldozing of their home and that your grandfather's in jail for nonpayment of taxes."

"How can they pay taxes when they aren't allowed to work and when their house, such as it was, was destroyed – by them?" he asked bitterly. "I'll start with the labs here, then.

"Nora and Ralph had a great idea about establishing a genetic research facility to try to beat the rest of the world to the secret of being able to raise certain crops in salt water. There were other things, but that was to be the first priority and most important project. Ralph was to get the financing and so forth, find something to use for a lab and hire a security force. Me. Nora would find the scientists. George was already known as a meticulous worker, so would be in charge of keeping the labs in order as well as doing research in his field, which is microbiotics.

"Nora hired Gus, who was beginning to get a good reputation. We all signed a contract to share equally in any profits except for fifteen percent, which would go to three investors. Ralph got Sylvia Marks, a woman he knew for years and who wanted to help him get started in something and Carson Wilder, a complete horse's ass who happened to have a lot more money than sense. I got my uncle to finish the funding because he would be willing to support anything that may someday lead our people out of this impossible vicious oppression. He was the one who suggested a lot of it to Ralph. He even suggested the kinds of research and said that we made the right decisions as to distribution of the findings – he does have a lot of connections over the entire East.

"Food is the one important thing in that entire area of the world. It's the weapons, the economy, the power – everything. If cheap and easy food can be grown two-thirds of the power the oppressors hold is gone. Sea water even has all the minerals and other fertilizers the plants need.

"Uncle Yusef even has connections in Spain and France and in South America and Africa, all places where the research has the greatest value and impact, though the Euromarket isn't nearly so important as the others. We would have the connections in place and waiting for us.

"Ralph had great dreams of making the discoveries that would free all peoples in all places. He was a truly good if overly idealistic person. We had already as much as agreed we would accept only enough to pay the investors a reasonable amount and to finance a few years' more research into other things for pure profit. We would, for the most part, give the world the results of the most important research ever undertaken!

"The world will never know how fine and honorable Ralph Meiner was. I swear to you that I would willingly give my own life if he could have lived to see the research completed and personally given it to the world. I swear I had nothing to do with...."

He stopped and choked back a sob. We waited a minute, then he went on. "Ralph found this building. We had the financing in place. The contractors were putting in the important labs. I installed the security system while Ralph ordered all the equipment and supplies we would need. We were a big, idealistic, happy family, all working toward a goal that was bigger than the bunch of us combined. Everything was perfect.

"Nora first developed an insert mechanism to make certain major food crops produce their own nitrogenous bacterial fixer nodules. It wasn't a huge thing, but it brought in some funds.

"Gus developed a resistant strain of lawn grass to the fungi that can ruin a lawn overnight in Florida. We made a little on that. It was working perfectly. Everything was on schedule.

"Nora made the first breakthrough step in the gene splice for salt resistance and we began building the roof facility. That's when the end really began for Gus.

"Gus and Ralph always argued about Israel. It was all goodnatured at first. Gus couldn't find anything wrong in anything Israel did, while Ralph was constantly decrying that they were becoming exactly what they most hated and feared. Gus saying we had learned a strong lesson from the war and gas chambers and that Israel must be strong, Ralph saying Israel had learned nothing or they would see that what they were doing was exactly what the Nazis did to become strong – and look what that led to!

"I changed my name when I was starting college. I'm darker than the others here, but I'm lighter than many Palestinians. My mother was half Iranian and half English. They neither one knew and I didn't tell them, though Ralph knew from my uncle and never said anything to Gus or the others. I made it a point not to get into those arguments because I would get mad and cause friction. I was willing to wait because our research could be the ultimate difference. It became the single most important thing in my life.

"Gus found a few tomato plants growing with their roots in a place where very high tides covered them, yet they had fruit and weren't hurt by the salt. The tomatoes weren't very tasty, but they tested safe and nutritious. Gus extracted the responsible gene sequence and started a strain of tomatoes, but the oarticular gene wasn't one that was transferable by insert, so it had to be done by hybridizing. All of a sudden the plants were gone, the research was gone – everything. Gus said he'd given the whole mess to Israel. We could have demanded compensation for it. The investors were actually guaranteed payment based on market value. It wasn't a huge thing, but it was worth enough to finance a good bit of research. There was a stink, but we finally agreed to forget it, but it wasn't to happen again.

"I suddenly didn't trust Gus. If he did that once he would damned well do it again. I placed the secondary recorders on the cameras so the comp sec system couldn't be breached without me catching it. It was an easy time to do it because Nora's lab was being finished and the wiring was mostly exposed already. All I had to do was run a fine secondary output wire from each camera to my office.

"Gus had taken to working in the vault a lot of the time. I checked the secondaries regularly from the day I finished putting the system in. The second night, two Israeli agents keyed the door and walked in. They went directly to the vault, stayed more than an hour and left. There was no record on the comp sec system.

"I didn't know how they did it, but the kid you and Mr. Jacobi brought did precisely the same thing. I would like to know how you did it. I can find a way to thwart it if I know....

"Nora's notes were kept in her office in a file cabinet. There were a lot of times when George was working around the place when the door was left opened to the offices and those agents went in one time when George was in the vault helping Gus do an inventory of the supplies. They photo-graphed all of Nora's notes.

"Suddenly Gus was ordering things much the same as Nora

was using. It was much too obvious. Gus and those spies had stolen Nora's research.

"I pointed out to Ralph that the tomato thing was never given to anyone, was in fact used only by the Israelis in one small secret plot where they were producing a lot of seed for their own use. In a single year they had enough – beyond doubt – to supply starters to everyone in the area, yet they did no such thing. They just kept a minimal test plot going to ensure fresh seed every season. Once again, something was obvious about their intentions as to sharing these things.

"Ten days ago Gus started gathering a lot of culture plates, lots of mericloning equipment and lots of embryo development staging materials. It was obvious he had made the breakthrough, somehow. I was sure he would announce it to us, but I wasn't sure I could keep silent that he had stolen the research from Nora. He didn't announce anything to anyone. He became more and more secretive. I heard him on the phone in his office through a bug I planted there telling Auermond to come to the lab, now, and to make arrangements to transport the research . That was about four thirty five in the afternoon. I decided to see for myself exactly what was going on. If that research was to be given to the same bunch of scum the tomatoes were....

"I made a plan right from the first time I first became suspicious, so I climbed into a carton marked for the vault on the loading ramp and George took it in on his regular rounds. I got out of the carton when he was gone and hid under the clone carrier unit. It's a large space where no one ever looks. I had my knife with me because I fully intended to kill him if he was actually going to sell us out – or give the research to my people's enemy to be used as another weapon against us.

"Gus came into the lab and wrote all his notes up carefully until Auermond came. About six o'clock. Gus was going to help pack all the embryos and cultures and they were going to sneak out of the country before dawn. There was a plane waiting. Auermond went to get Shartz and the truck. He would be back in twenty minutes.

"I came out, confronted Gus, then knifed him after stunning him with the butt of the knife. I took the notes and tapes that had any relevance. I hung a note in Aramic on the knife that said, 'Traitors die. It is the will of Allah' and left, after putting the cultures and clones back where the Israelis wouldn't be able to find them. I left, took the notes and tapes to hide under the back seat in my car and excised myself from the records when I came back in before going to the vault to 'discover' the body.

"You know everything since then except how I felt when I saw the knife was gone and the note was gone. There was a ridiculous little scalpel in the wound!

"Later I put the notes and tapes on Nora's car seat and checked the secondary camera VCRs after the place was cleared out. Auermond left with my knife and the note in his hand. I almost told you all of this when Ralph was killed. I think it's obvious who killed him."

"You have the tape of that?" Len demanded. "Auermond with the knife in his hand?"

Vore went out of the room and returned after about five or six minutes with a tape. He dropped it in the playback, ran it to a certain spot and put it on the screen:

Shartz came from the rear door with a dolly. Auermond followed and they went directly to the secure vault, slid a cardkey in the slot and went in. They came back out less than a minute later. Shartz was pushing the dolly as fast as he could go. Auermond was right behind him with a curved bronze knife in his hand with the note sticking between his fingers. I could read his lips. I learned that on a recent case. He was saying, "Hurry the fuck up! This is a trap! We can't let them find us here!"

I picked up the phone and called Tony.

"I want you to locate Shartz and Auermond. Now! I'm going after them with everything I've got, personally."

"I can find out where they are at any time. What you got? You're not half-cocked are you?"

I told him about the tape with Auermond leaving with the knife in his hand.

"But why would they kill Gus? He change his mind about giving them the stuff?"

"No. Ed killed Gus. He's told us about it. He didn't kill Ralph. He had the tapes from the secondary hidden in the little kitchen where no one would look for them. I thought it was just a little too easy to get rid of those agents."

"What you gonna do?"

"I want to ask Ed a few questions, then I'll go after those two. They aren't going to get away with this, Tony. I mean that! If I have to drug them to get their miserable asses out of Israel that's what I'll do – and screw Israel and this lousy crooked damned administration here!"

"They aren't going to go anywhere near Israel. Israel doesn't need their type around to muck things up. They've got enough trouble with all those military experts training the drug dealers in Colombia. They can't take a hell of a lot more publicity of this type."

"It's falling apart over there isn't it? This is anarchy. It's as bad as the North thing. Everybody's going off on their own tangents and no one knows what the hell's going on."

"It's decay all right. I'll have whatever you need ready immediately. Last I heard, the agents were headed for England."

I hung up and turned back to Vore. "Tell me about your Uncle Yusef. I have to know how he fits into all this."

"I informed him about all of it. He didn't know anything except that I was watching Eisingstein very closely because

I thought he was going to pull a fast one. Yusef knew I intended to kill Gus if he really did try that kind of thing. He said he'd do all he could to protect me.

"My uncle didn't have anything to do with this part. He was always making plans to get new arms to Israel's enemies and he handles things to raise funds for the PLO and a few other organizations, but his parents are still there, so he doesn't dare do anything that could cause reprisals against them."

"They would never do anything to his parents for something *he* did!" Len said. "They aren't like that! That's the kind of thing the Nazis did to *them*!"

"What? You don't read the newspapers?" Ed asked sarcastically. "Maybe you only read the parts you want to read? They bulldozed down my grandparent's home for no reason! They shoot eight and ten year old kids! What does it take to make you see what they are? All this crap in the papers about a shipload of Jews who were turned away in the forties – and now you turn away Palestinian refugees from the same things because Israel is a friendly power? They send spies against this country, the single country who actually supports them economically? They bomb their neighbors because the neighbors might get some weapons to defend themselves? They jail people such as my grandfather because they can't pay the taxes used to support the soldiers who do these things to them – yet they're not doing anything wrong? They defy the UN and they defy this country on civil and human rights, but they're better than the Nazis?

"You *can't* be that stupid! This country's government is no better than Israel's Mussolini and you know it! We're the *only* support Israel has in the UN. Even England, who's almost always with us there, won't countenance our votes!"

"Don't say it, Len," I warned. "We aren't concerned with the political situation over there. We're concerned with a murder here. I don't agree with all that Ed's saying, but I've learned enough that I can't deny most of it. I see it differently in that it's a minority of the Israelis who're doing it. A hell of a lot of them are like Ralph and are fighting it, themselves. The agents who committed the murder here aren't actually representatives of Israel itself, they're only representatives of a small faction who are hardliners."

"The simple facts are staring you in the face," Ed said. "A majority of them elected those hardliners. They have *spies* here! They have been censored by every single country in the entire world *except* the US! The bulldozings and the murders of children are in the news almost every night. They censor the news. They refuse to allow our news reporters into the areas where they do these things – and we meekly say, `Yes Sir! Anything you say, Sir! We'll kiss your royal ass, Sir!'

"So why not add a few billion to their aid package? That'll show them exactly where we stand! It'll show the world!"

Len started to say something, then shrugged. Last night's news told about the "unfortunate" deaths of an eight year old girl and a ten year old boy. Even Len wouldn't try to justify using live bullets against children throwing rocks. It would be totally pointless to try to change the way Vore thought, even if he could think of anything to say in rebuttal. He would have said something about terrorists, but the reply that those were exactly the tactics Israel was using would negate anything he could say and he knew it.

"We have to charge you with the killing of Gus. If you can prove he was going to deal with foreign agents, friendly or not, you can probably beat the worst charges unless you get a stacked jury.

"If you can prove the thing about the tomatoes you've given full justification for your fears. Those were the same agents he gave the tomato seeds to?"

"Yes. I have all of it on tape and some of that transaction

is audio as well as video. He admitted to the whole thing in Ralph's office in front of the cameras there. It's against the law to give this kind of technology to any foreign power without clearance from Washington. There are plenty of agencies in this country who would give this to Israel and everyone else."

"Well, I'm heading for England, I guess," I said. "Tony says that Auermond and Shartz are there. I'll try to find a way to get them back to Florida. If I can get them back here Len can grab them and we can fry their asses.

"Guard the tape of Auermond with that knife with your life!"

"Before you go, CD," Len said. "Will you object if I arrange for Vore to stay here on his own recognizance? I think that will give you a powerful lever with Auermond and Shartz."

"What do you have in mind?"

"If you were to be able to get word out that Ed had that tape? He was going to use it? You could maybe let them know he has all the tapes and that they've put Israel in an untenable situation? Maybe they'll believe there were voice-coder audio bugs in the secure vault. They'll compromise Israel itself because of the claims they've made?

"I'm saying this in front of you, Ed, because you're going to be bait in a trap. They're killers – and they have training in things I haven't even dreamed of. I can only guarantee to *try* to protect you."

"I can actually dummy some audio tapes. I can get a computer voice-match through synthesis. I only need a few sentences for them to work with. I have Eisingstein's print on file."

"JK will work with you," I said. "I'll make it first priority to get something recorded and will send it to you. I can use a voicecoder from Crane."

"You can computer-send it to Tony on the Crane secret lines can't you?" Len asked.

"You can digitalize it and send it fax on a phone line," Ed suggested.

"I'll have Tony and JK meet me at the airport with the special equipment and use instructions. Ed isn't going to be running anywhere, I think. If he's willing, I am."

"It's settled," Ed said, simply.

I used the phone in the car to call Tony, then went home to get my stuff together. I would use a disguise I made when I was on a case awhile back to meet the Israeli agents. They wouldn't recognize me. I'd also get some things from a good friend of Gramps who was retired from New Scotland Yard. I was busily formulating a plan as I drove. I hoped it would prove practical.

I called Mike at the airport and told him to get the jet ready and see it was serviced for international. As soon as I got to the house I called my friend in London to arrange for the trip. The visa was still good in my passport, but I'd need other identification over there if I was to pull it off.

"Have the identification under the name of ... Geof Hartington Fortesque," I requested of Sir William – my ex-CID friend, Chief Inspector William Hopkins, rtd. "I have a lot of stuff with that name on it. We can add the pictures and prints as soon as I get there."

"We have pictures," he said. "It can be here and waiting. All official-looking and all that rot (He really does talk like that! It's not only in the movies!), don't you know."

"Believe me, I won't look anything like the pictures you might have. I'll walk in and you can see if you recognize me. If you do we'll have to change me more. Those two are trained in that kind of thing."

"Oh, I'll notice you, Old Sock! I'm trained to notice things, too, you know. I was good at it if I do say so myself!"

"We'll see! It'll be early tomorrow sometime. See you then."

"Tally-ho! Knock me up first thing. Room two ten, the Grand. You have the number."

We hung up soon and I took the disguise out. I'd put it on after I got there or I wouldn't look enough like my legitimate passport photos to pass customs. I told Alma and the kids goodbye and headed for the airport. Tony met me and we discussed where the two were staying and all he'd found out about them. They actually worked for a radical Zionist group in Israel, not directly for the government, but we'd guessed that. They were personas non gratas in Israel now because the country had been embarrassed enough lately and didn't need anything like this. Tony gave me a small digital recorder and showed me how to use it. He had JK with him and had hooked up a player to the radio in the jet.

"You get the tape on the recorder," JK said. "It doesn't play, it only records. Put the tape in here and broadcast through the international hookup to CraneCo at extension eleven forty one, Sarasota branch. That's Tony's office. I'll have everything there and ready. Vore's going to come to the plant to make reco tapes and we can enhance from the tapes he has on video. You said you read Auermond's lips on that one tape so we'll show him that one with vocals. I'll get some lip readers to get the stuff from the other tapes where we can. Once we have that we can do pretty much what we want."

"The stuff will never be needed in court. It won't matter that it won't actually match a voice print. It's just for bait in a trap."

"It'll make a better voiceprint match than any actual audio tape ever could," JK replied. "We'll actually be working *from* a voiceprint!"

He got a blank look and wandered away. Tony shook his head, grinned and shrugged.

I said my goodbyes, climbed aboard, got clearance and was off.

I rented a hotel room in the Grand, took my suitcases up and spent almost two hours putting on the disguise. I had red hair, red muttonchops, a neat red beard, a small pot belly, walked with a cane over my arm, was a bit loudmouthed in a higher pitch than my normal voice and was somewhat pigeon-toed. I was freckled and had very green eyes.

The hair was actually mine, dyed, coated at the base with some special gunk, cut off and saved and glued back on. The freckles were made by using a whiter makeup and removing the spots with a special acidic solution to let the natural tan show through, the pot was a prosthetic that was good enough to fool a professional detective who knew me, the voice was a device I wore behind my teeth, the eye color was contacts – the one thing that really irritated and bothered me – and the walk was shaped soles and heels on the shoes so everything was automatic and natural.

I studied myself in the mirror. It really was good!

I went down to the lobby and strolled around a few minutes, then bought a London newspaper, sat in a plush chair and had a cup of complimentary (awful) coffee while I read what was going on in the world from a slightly different point of view than we had in the states. The African famines were somewhat lessened, but there was still a lot of starvation and disease. That had died in popularity back home. I didn't remember hearing anything about it in months.

There was plenty salt water along the coast. Tomatoes were highly nutritious. I wondered how many would be alive right now if those people had a few seeds for the past two years. I wondered if the new process would come in time to stop that from ever happening again. I wondered if someone like those I was looking for were to get the process first if they would ever have it.

I read the rest of the paper, then sat, thinking. Sir William came from the left, walked a few feet from me and went into the restaurant. I waited about five minutes, then strolled in to sit at the next table to order ham and eggs. He looked around the room at intervals, several times he looked directly at me. I finally managed to look up precisely as he looked at me and met his eyes.

"Oi saigh!" I exclaimed. "Would you have any ketchup? They ditn't bring me any and Oi cahn't eat aigs without!"

"Tomato sauce on eggs? Odd, don't you know.

"You're not from England?"

"Belize, Myte! Oi'm here to knock back a lesson or two at New Scotland Yard. Been to France for the Interpol, Myte. Bloody neat-o!"

"Going into police work, are you? Did a spot of police work myself. Retired from the force, matter of fact! Got to keep up with the field nowadays or it'll leave you so far behind you don't know where you are. Computers do everything, it seems. I imagine they don't have so many computers there, do they?"

"Oh, we don't have that much croime of toipes what needs comps in Belize. Big Yank companies own everything. Get a few petty thieves and a murder now and again, but Oi'm in training for the smuggeling end. Oi could tell you a thing or two what goes staitesoide in cola boxes!"

"With that druggie situation in the states I don't think I'd care to get involved in that end of it," Sir William said, with a shudder. "Not that long since, we didn't even carry pistols here except on special assignment. I was CID, so I usually had one about. Most times I didn't bother to carry it unless something was expected, you see."

"C Oi D? Bloody interesting! You maike any graide, Myte?"

"Well, yes. I was Chief Inspector, international jewels and art department! Had one case where there was a connection in Belize. Ring working out of Hawaii. Worked with a fellow from the states, matter of fact. He's to meet me today. Name of Grimes. Know him?"

"Groimes? Very common naime, Oi'm afraid, eh what? The only Groimes Oi cahn remember was a rahther stroiking woman naime of Alma Groimes. Gathering orchids. Had the hubby along, sorry to saigh. Fabulous woman!"

"That was my friend, CD, and his wife," Sir William said, very stiffly. "She is a striking woman. I can assure you she would act no differently if her husband was there or not!"

"Oh! Oi saigh! Oi ditn't mean any least dispairity Oi assure you! Everything was poifectly proper at all toimes, Chief Inspector! Oi can dream, cahn't oi?"

He grinned. "I must say, she makes any man dream!

"My name's Bill. William J. Hopkins, CID retired."

"Oi'm Geof," I said, watching him spin his head to stare at me with his mouth hanging wide open. "Geof Hartington Fortesque, at your service!"

"I'll be damned! I wouldn't have believed you could do it! How can you control your voice so well at that pitch and timbre?"

I moved over to sit at his table with him. No one was very close, so I slipped the device out from behind my teeth. "This thing does most of it, so I don't have to worry about the tone or pitch, but I have to be careful of my phrasing and accent. I sound more Aussie than Belize."

I slipped the thing back behind my teeth.

"I know how the shoes make you walk distinctly. The makeup's as good as I've ever seen. I hope that's an artificial beer belly! I'd hate to think you'd let yourself go that much, but I must say it's well done!"

"It's a disguise I've used before. You can see why I said the pictures would have to be done here."

We chatted about various things through the breakfast, then went to have photos taken and processed.

I now had a very official-looking ID that said I was a special CID agent working with Interpol on international terrorism. We went to New Scotland Yard for the ID things where Sir William introduced me to the people I didn't know from former trips.

We finally went into the office of the present chief inspector in charge of terrorism. Sir William introduced a dark man with curly black hair and a hawk nose – and eyes that would record better than a camera. I *knew* those eyes didn't miss any detail, no matter how small.

"Nigel Birnbaum, our Chief Inspector," Sir William said. "You know of CD and his grandfather, Nige. You can see from those pictures why he said not to use them."

Nigel had a man bring a pot of coffee, then leaned back to study me.

"Tell us about it," Sir William said. "If Nigel feels your case has merit you get the papers, though you must be warned! The yard will claim no knowledge of those papers if it comes to that! This is to be unlike what your grandfather did. This time we're to know what you're doing and why *before* you do it. We agreed with him in reality, but would have been forced to refuse, officially.

"So! Who are these mad terrorists you're after? PLO? Syrians? Who?"

"Israelis," I replied, bracing for the explosion.

"Ah, yes! I didn't think you Yanks would admit there were any such," Nigel said.

Chapter seven

I rented a small car, hooked up the little recorder hidden in my pot belly prosthetic and checked the roadmap Sir William and Nigel had marked for me. I had to drive over to a place called Leepstead Under Hamilton and find a "country" place called The Three Larches. Nigel and Sir William seemed to assume I wouldn't have any trouble finding it. Tony said the Israeli agents were staying there as guests of the owners, Mort Solomon and his wife, Cleo.

"Mort's always been a bit of the extreme radical," Nigel had explained. "Gets into causes. Ran for parliament, but didn't get enough of the vote to make him try that again. Cleo's a flighty type. Overdid the LSD in the seventies and still acts like a Yank hippie. She grows herbs and spices all over the place, casts horoscopes and makes incense. We once discovered *Lophophora williamsii* in one of her rock gardens, which she said she thought was only another cute little cactus, but we all knew bloody damned well she knew peyote when she saw it. I don't doubt there's canabis growing there and even those mushrooms, but she only uses them herself, so we leave her alone. There's not much more mental damage that can happen to her unless she's a better actress than I think she is. You never really know.

"Mort's sharp. He can be pretty likeable, but he's shrewd at the same time, if you know what I mean. We keep an eye on that one, but he's too slippery. We don't know what he's up to, but I'll bet it's no good! There's no way he could live the high way he does on the income from his little insurance agency. He's a fanatic Zionist, so he's not popular in the area."

That's what I knew about them. Now I was driving across some rather picturesque countryside on my way to try to scam two spies into returning to the US to try to cover their own backsides. I didn't care what Solomon and his wife were or what they were doing. I warned Nigel and Sir William about what those people were doing in the states, but England wouldn't put up with it in quite the same way. They'd be much more careful how they acted there.

I was surprised when I arrived into the picturesque sleepy farming village of Leepstead Under Hamilton. It was so typical of the tourist brochures I'd seen describing elegant country life in rural England I couldn't believe it, but there were no touristy businesses. There wasn't even an inn. The only restaurant was mostly a tea room. I stopped at the only petrol station and asked about a place to stay overnight.

"Ain't no place here," the attendant said around his pipe. "People goes on to Hamilton. Got a motor hotel 'n everthin there. Reg'lar city now. Done growed up some since the road went through 'round 'bout ten years ago. Fancy-smancy place. Bunch a high-falutin' snobs, you aks me! Six'r so kilometers away 'n they thinks they's in another world, they do! Bringin' in those credit card things! I don't take 'em! I pays cash 'n I accepts cash. Don't need no high-falutin' plastic money 'round hereabouts!

"You Aussie? Ain't from 'round hereabouts!"

"Oi'm from Belize, Myte. Come here to study at the Yard. Work with them and Interpol, you know."

"Bunch 'a Frog fops in that there Interpol thing, I hears. They want ta run everthin' in the Market. Don't need 'em here!"

I sighed and said the world was changing and not often for the better. He agreed vehemently and I asked about The Three Larches and its inhabitants.

"Fin'ly got somethin' on the bloody Yids, did ya? Know'd they was inter somethin' crooked all along! Bunch 'a bloody revolutionary radicals! Don't need 'em here! Fits better in Hamilton, they does! She's got no sense an' he's a sharp one, he is! Better off fer all'n us if they was all locked up! Don't need 'em here!"

I made a neutral comment and he said the place was off the South Road about a kilometer and a half.

"Got cows. Six or seven mebbe. Just pets – 'n that silly girl makes some butter. Cows is too old, but they don't eat red meat.

"Stupid! Him allus preachin' 'bout killin' off all the Germans an' A-rabs! Believes in killin' *people*, but don't believe in killin' *cows*! Don't need 'em here!"

I made my escape and headed out the side road he indicated. There was a small sign on a long tree-lined drive that said, "Larches," so I went down it.

The house was one of those enormous gray stone manor house things, probably a couple of hundred years old. It was maintained in excellent condition, but the grounds were planted in haphazard plots. There were several decrepit cows moping around on a low fenced pasture to one side and a large open meadow running down a small hill to a stream on the other. The drive went to the front of the house.

I parked beside a Mercedes, across from a huge wooden door. There was a pickup truck next to the Mercedes and a BMW past that a few feet. A woman of about thirty five came out the doors before I was out of the car. She was dressed in a wild madras skirt that hung to the ground, an electric green tightfitting blouse and cheap bangles and strings of beads hanging all over her. There were rings on all her fingers – two on some, mostly made of silver and turquoise. She had wild black hair that was long and straight and seemed to float along behind her. She was slim, but with a shape – not stick-thin like the models – and was really graceful in her movements. When she got close I could see she was just between "pretty" and "beautiful." Very close to beautiful.

"Oh! Oi saigh now! Do Oi have the distinct pleasure of

addressing Mrs. Cleopatra Solomon? Oi hope!"

"It's just Cleo. It's not short for anything. You shouldn't use the 'Mrs.' with the given name of the wife. I'm Cleo Solomon, or Mrs. Mort Solomon – like you give a shit!

"You would do well to stop eating meat and drinking so much beer. You're not healthy.

"You have to be Pisces with Venus waning. It won't do any good to tell you anything because you always run around with your mind made up about everything. Very unlucky in love. Lousy in bed. Way too egocentric.

"You don't believe one word of it, so you're not here for a reading. Mort's in the study and his two creepy friends are in the back terrace room. Should I know you?"

"No. Oi'm just here to talk to a Mr. Auermond and a Mr. Shartz about some ... things. Oi imagine they'll be the creepy ones, don't you know. Oi'm with Interpol. Need to let them know moi oi's on them! Maide a roight mess back in the staites, they did!

"Oi'm Taurus, don't you know. Don't believe any of that rot, anyhow nowdais!"

"Ha-ah! You walk Pisces and you talk Pisces and your attitude is Pisces! Nah-ah!There's been some mix-up. You must be adopted and they screwed up the papers. I'm never wrong!"

"Oi *was* adopted!" I said, putting a little awe in my voice and look. "That's roight amaizing, but Oi know moi birthdaite. Certificaite, don't you know."

She grinned and said, "A piece of paper says just what someone writes on it. You were a bit young to be able to correct it, now weren't you? You got a name?"

"Oh, Oi'm sorry. Oi'm Geof Hartington Fortesque. Oi was born just Geof Hartington ahnd was adopted when Oi was fresh orphaned at one year of aige by the Fortesque family bahck in Belize."

"Belize? In Central America? That explains the screwup in the paperwork with your birth certificate.

"INTERPOL?! You're from INTERPOL?"

"Er, yes. Here to see Mr. Auermo...."

"I *knew* it! I *knew* they were creeps! You can get them out of here!

"What did they do?"

"Oi'm not sure they ditn't kill someone."

"Hah! I knew it! I'm never wrong!" she cried happily, and went on down the drive and over to the pasture. I went around the house to the terrace room where Auermond and Shartz were sitting at a table with a pile of papers and maps in front of them. They looked up as I entered.

"Mr.s Auermond and Shartz, Oi presume? Oi'm Geof Fortesque from New Scotland Yard, working terrorism with Interpol. Our informaition told me you would be here.

"Oi'm here to notify you we keep the roight royal oi on the two of you proizes! Oi don't know quoite everything you two did bahck staitesoide, but what Oi do know is it's causing quoite the stir, don't you know. Bloke says he's going to have you extradoited for espionahge against the staites. Flaimin' good to see you gone!

"Oi thought Oi'd tell you we won't let you out of our soight, don't you know. Spoi against the Yanks and you'll do the egzact saime here. Difference is, we won't let you get awaigh with it!"

"What are you talking about?" Auermond snapped. "How the hell would.... This is crazy! We're just tourists! We aren't *spies*!"

"Not what Oi heard! Bloke has it all on video, don't you know. Troying to get Interpol in on it. Saighs you're Israeli spoies ahnd he can prove it. Says you're terrorists, too. That's whoi Oi'm called in."

"Damn! Grimes is just mad because we beat him in a

business deal!" Auermond cried. "He doesn't have any videos of us! He doesn't have any such thing! It's a phony frameup!"

"Oi don't know anything about any Groimes, you know. Our informaition is from some secret laboratory security man. Clearances and all that rot, don't you know. Interpol's woiking on what we call doirect informaition from the poison. Seem he guarantees to produce the evidence when we deliver you to the staites. There's no Groimes in moi report, only an E. Vore."

"But I don't see how he could have any recordings of any type concerning us!" Shartz cried. "We haven't even been to any such place! Where is this secret laboratory?"

"Oi only have the informaition they gaive me. Oi'm to tell you extradition papers maigh soon be soigned and your country will be embarrassed. Oi don't think Israel can stahnd much more flaimin' embairrassment, don't you know. Bloody bad scene, what?"

"You haven't seen these alleged videos?" Auermond asked.

"Oi think they use rahther special machinery. Mr. Vore will show them when you're returned to the staites. He's been cleared through Interpol special security as a special informaition agent, so they'll operaite on his woid, don't you know. Special agent, sworn oath and all that rot. Only man aloive to have ever seen it yet, but Oi'd bet he can produce it! Wants to faice you with it. Saighs to tell you Ralph was a friend of his if we foind you. Saighs you're going to paigh most dearly. Oi hear he wants to faice you in poison for some reason. Saighs there's a video of Mr. Auermond with what he refers to as `The knoife' in his hand. Saighs the videos of the vault are all so very valuable in the caise against you.

"Oi think there was a murder and Oi think you did it. Oi also think you're terrorists, because there were two people killed there – both Jews. Oi think Mr. Solomon and his woife are in some dainger here. Oi think you'd best know we'll be watching you very cairefully! Oi also think that, should any accidents befall Mr. or Mrs. Solomon, you will foind we at the Yard know a thing or two about how to handle such as you! There won't be any namby-pamby deals and traides with an embassy. Oi'll see you shot, Oi will! Oi'll personally see it! Oi'd further suggest you two proizes leave the UK and taike all vacations elsewhere in future! Do Oi make moiself *quoite clear*?"

"If I were in as bad a shape as you are, I'd be very careful about making threats," Shartz said through his teeth.

"Ahnd Oi'd be most careful about a poison deliberaitely being deceptive in his poisonal appearance before Oi offered challenge!" I said through my own teeth. "You moight just foind Oi've had some training that doesn't show. You moight foind that to be very deliberaite. You moight just foind Oi'd loike very much for you to lift a hahnd to me! Oi'll be watching you."

I turned and walked out. Now it would be up to them. If this was handled right they would be calling Ed Vore. I hoped Solomon had some kind of surveillance device in that terrace room. It would be nice for him to become afraid to have them there.

I drove back into Hamilton and got a room at the motel. In the morning I would make it a point to be noticed from a distance, watching The Three Larches. I wanted to make them get increasingly nervous. I planned to see they became much more nervous every hour they stayed around.

In the morning I got a call from Sir William, who said the Yard received an inquiry from a place called The Three Larches about an Interpol agent. Nigel took the call and said there was indeed an agent named Geof Fortesque on special assignment with Interpol and the Yard from Belize, C. A., but no further information was available or would become available in the foreseeable future. Citizens were asked to cooperate with the police in the ever-ongoing investigation into criminal blah, blah, blah.

I drove to the house to find the BMW gone. Cleo was working in the rock garden by the kitchen door and a dark man I assumed was Mort Solomon came out to talk to her, so I could assume Auermond and Shartz had taken the BMW for a drive. I went back to the motel, then back to The Larches later in the afternoon, but the BMW was still gone. I called Sir William when I got back to the motel in the early evening. The BMW never returned.

"I couldn't reach you earlier," Sir William said. "You can come on back in. Your Mr. Auermond and Mr. Shartz are now staying at the Airport Hotel. They came to Heathrow about two hours ago and immediately booked a flight to Tampa International Airport, Tampa, Florida, USA. They leave tomorrow at one thirty PM.

"Nigel had a good spot-trace from that Larches place. There was a call to a Mr. E. Vore in Sarasota, Florida, USA late last evening. He spoke to them for almost seven minutes."

"What about?"

"We didn't have audio, only the call trace," Sir William said. "He called the overseas information operator, got Vore's number from the directory in Sarasota, then placed the call.

"You're to call a Mr. Tony Jacobi at Crane Sarasota as quickly as possible on a secure line. Important."

We chatted for a few minutes, then I got in the car and headed for London. I had to know what they discussed with Ed Vore and I wanted to see exactly what Tony had. It might be connected. Tony and JK were working with Vore.

I used the scrambler unit on my jet secure comphone, sent the recordings of Auermond and Shartz's voices, then had Tony paged. He came on to say, "Get back here as fast as you can. Auermond called Ed."

"I think I scared hell out of them. I told them about the videos. I sort of hinted about the `great value' of the recordings so as to let them believe that Vore would sell them the evidence."

"I wish you'd have let me know what you were going to tell them. I had to improvise – or Ed did.

"Did you tell them Interpol was on it and that Ed had tapes of all the stuff that could only be played on his own equipment?"

"Something on that order. I was vague. I'll leave here in about an hour. I want to beat them back. They won't leave here until tomorrow afternoon sometime."

"Leave there?" Tony asked. "What do you mean?"

"You didn't know that they booked passage to Tampa tomorrow? Isn't that what Ed arranged?"

"Ed arranged to get all the stuff together and to be ready to deliver it to them Sunday – that's three days – in Miami. They'll give him one million dollars in small old bills. He's blackmailing them."

"He'd be dead by Sunday. We're going to have a little surprise waiting for those two proizes."

"Proizes?"

"Prizes, as intoned by one Geof Hartington Fortesque," I replied. I could picture Tony giving the phone the finger.

I went back to the Yard, told Nigel what happened and gave him the phony papers back, then went to the hotel, where I removed the disguise and talked with Sir William. I was in the air shortly, heading back to Sarasota.

"Cal has an operative waiting to follow them when they get into Tampa International," Len said, pouring us each a cup of the special gourmet coffee Alma blends for him. "The FHP can have four different people following him at different times. They shouldn't be suspicious about that to any great degree."

"I'm gonna talk with that woman who uses the comps here," JK said and wandered out. Tony grinned and shrugged.

"They'll get into Tampa late tonight. It wasn't a direct flight. That'll give them all day tomorrow to do something before Vore's supposed to meet them in Miami Sunday morning."

"The way I see it, they'll head directly over to my place, thinking I have the videos and tapes there," Ed said. "We'll have them right there!"

"We'll set something up," Tony said. "JK's already wired your place. We'll have to record them actually doing something criminal here for Len to be able to act. If they're inside the house he's got them, so JK and I took a crew from Crane and installed a few interesting little gimmicks.

"There was a buzz from Len's phone. He picked it up and handed it to me.

"CD? Bill here," Sir William said. "I'm at Nigel's CID office. He said I should contact you to inform you that Auermond got on the plane with someone, but it wasn't Shartz. Shartz went back to The Larches. There was also a long distance international call from Auermond to Sarasota, Florida, last evening. We don't know who he called. Left it for you, you see, as you're there.

"There seems to be a foul odor from a country north of here!"

We talked a few minutes, then hung up. Len picked up the phone and called a friend in the Sarasota Police Department, argued a minute, then called the state. He argued with them and slammed the phone down.

"What's the matter?" Tony asked.

"Stupid goddamned idiots won't tell me the number or address Auermond called from London! See if I help *them* next time they need our equipment!"

Tony grinned and went out. I suggested Len try calling the international operator and looking for a way to get the information directly when Tony came back in with JK. JK looked at the phone, then at the fax machine, then at the computer console Len used to make reports. He shook his head and wandered out of the office. Tony said not to worry about getting the number, but to wait. Three minutes later JK came back in, asked Len if he could use his seat, plugged his computer power supply in, attached a modem line to the phone and another to the fax machine and punched a few keys.

Some figures came up on the screen. He punched a long digital code. After a few minutes of playing with the board and getting replies the fax machine printed a list of numbers, dates, and times.

"That's as close as I can get it," JK said. "Those are all the calls from London to Sarasota in the past twenty four hours."

"How did you do that!?" Len cried.

"Er, just accessed the time and charges," JK answered. "All the hotels do it so they can know what to charge the guests for calls. It doesn't matter which company they go through because it's all billed through the satellites so it all goes through the main international recordkeeper computers to be billed automatically.

"You want CD's local bank statement to the minute? All I do is get access to the main credit clearinghouse and ask the right ... question ... if I know an account number ... I do ... Ah! Here it is!"

The fax machine said that I had one hundred nine million six hundred eleven thousand four hundred sixteen dollars and thirty three cents in cash at the moment with that bank. JK blushed and grinned, then unplugged his comp and wandered out. Tony grinned and shrugged. I laughed. Len laid his head on his desk blotter and groaned. "God! I'm supposed to arrest that damned kid on at least ten thousand felony charges for that!" he cried when he looked up and stopped laughing. "Great Scot! Nobody has any secrets at all anymore, even with their banks!"

"Not since the records are kept on computer," Tony agreed. "There's probably not another person in the US who could do it that easily."

"JK!" I yelled. "Can you come here a minute, please?"

He came back and looked quizzical.

"What are we making at the Tolsin plant?"

"I don't know if you even have a plant in, what did you say? Tolsin? I guess it's some kind of top secret crap for the pentagon or something."

"Could you find out with the comps?"

He looked confused, then got a strange grin on his face. Len pointed to a phone on a table outside the door, then picked up the fax list, tore off my bank statement, said "Lend me about fifty million, CD!" and threw it away.

He looked at the list of numbers.

"I wish I knew what the London number is and we'd know which one we're looking for," Len sighed. "I guess we can use a process of elimination."

"I looked up the Airport Hotel's number before I left London," I said. "I was going to have Geof call them, but thought better of it. Here."

I dug through my pockets and handed him the notepad with the hotel's main switchboard number on it.

"Five five five oh seven nine three," Len said.

I picked up the phone and dialed the number.

"Wilder residence."

"This is Morton Schlumm," I said, thinking fast. "Is Carson in?"

"Mr. Carson is attending a board meeting in Tampa and will not return today. He will be home on Monday from nine to four thirty."

Tampa, huh? By the airport maybe? I thanked her and said there was no message. It was about the orchid society's show next month.

"Carson Wilder?" Len asked. "What the hell is this?!"

"I think we'd better get hold of a complete dossier on Mr. Wilder!" I suggested. "Things are fitting a little better now. I was wondering how anyone as inept as he seemed to be could amass the amount of money I saw around his place. He couldn't have made that much investing in places he kept no watch on and he was 'way too `Oh, gee! I didn't have any idea!' about the labs. He was a bit too indignant that I would ask him the questions any detective would ask anyone who was concerned in a murder investigation. It's been gnawing at me ever since I went over there.

"Yusef knew about the labs, but only recently. Since the theft of Nora's work, as a matter of fact."

"I told him about that," Ed threw in.

"The one who killed – or ordered the death of – Ralph Meiner had to have a reason to do that," I continued. "Ralph Meiner got Wilder to invest, yet everyone seems to think Wilder's a royal pain in the ass if Ed's views are shared (Ed nodded). It didn't begin to figure. Ralph wasn't the kind to go after Wilder's type – simply *because* he would be a pain. Was the original plan to only have two investors, Ed?"

"Well, I did ... you're right! Ralph would get Sylvia, who always wanted to help him in some project, because she had loads of money and no one to spend it on or leave it to. Uncle Yusef wanted to invest to help our people. Ralph came in one day and announced he had another investor who would give us a cushion in operating funds. None of us thought much of it, at the time."

"The way I see it, Wilder found out about the type of research they were into, knew it was literally worth a billion dollars if it were sold to Israel and got in on the ground floor," Len said knowingly.

"He's the one who got the Israeli agents in on it!" Ed cried. "Ralph knew it had to be him, so he had Auermond kill Ralph to shut him up before he said anything! My god! He planned to kill Ralph all along! If Israel actually got this stuff when Gus ran off it would still be enough to hang Wilder because it would *still* be plain he was the one who was behind it! Only Ralph knew that Wilder was the contact!"

"You're probably right," I agreed. "Wilder intended to kill Ralph as soon as the deal was completed. Auermond already had his orders and it was suddenly more critical than ever to get rid of Ralph quickly. Auermond is smart. He went into that vault, found Gus dead and knew it was falling apart and that Ralph could be expected to add it up within hours. He would finger Wilder and Wilder would finger Auermond. He already had orders to get rid of Meiner. He just did it as soon as he had a chance. That phone call from London was a stupid mistake to make from either standpoint. *Very* unprofessional! They panicked."

"He couldn't know we would ever find out about it or that we could find who he called if we did," Len pointed out.

"He knew all about computer snooping," Tony argued. "He knew enough about it to work Ed's security system to his own advantage – and *that's* very advanced knowledge. Spies are trained in using machines of all types to do their work for them. He didn't know about JK, though. He didn't think we could get it without court orders to international phone companies. He would have time to cover his tracks. That means he doesn't have any idea least whatever about us knowing he's here. He thinks we're probably using Ed, but he isn't to meet Ed until Sunday – so far as we know. He would kill Ed and be gone by Sunday. We wouldn't have a chance of catching him!

"Well, we've got a few surprises of our own," Len said. "I think we'll have a lot of people trying to cover their tracks after tomorrow night."

"Tomorrow morning," I said. "They won't know if Ed plans to leave for Miami tomorrow afternoon. They'll come in and handle him directly. Their flight gets to Tampa about ten thirty PM. They can make it to Ed's place by two o'clock AM and be back in Tampa by five AM if the search for the stuff takes a long time and they have to wreck his whole place I wonder if JK can find if they've already booked a flight out of Tampa?"

"That doesn't matter," Len said. "They won't be taking it."

I was dying to know what kinds of things Tony and JK had done, but I wasn't about to let them know it. This was the kind of game Tony and I played with one another all the time. I would make him wonder what I was doing and he would do the same. I could count on it being rather spectacular.

"Speaking of JK," Tony said, "he's had almost half an hour to find what that plant's doing. I don't think twenty people in the world know what it is. It's sectioned. I can only tell you if he's right or wrong.

"Do you know, CD?"

"Pretty closely. I don't know if they've made any progress since we started this case. I only mentioned that plant because it's as top secret as anything this country's involved in, any-where."

"A hundred bucks says he'll find it in less than one hour!" Tony said.

"No takers! There's probably a simple way to find it."

We discussed deployment of personnel for about ten minutes, then JK came to the door. "Have they really found a way to do that?"

Tony grinned and shrugged. Len raised an eyebrow and said, "Do what?"

"Oh, that. The company's making a laser-activated fusion engine to drive a spaceship on interplanetary explorations," JK said matter-of-factly. "It should make it possible to deliver large payloads to say, Mars, and return with a cargo in about two days. Three if we're wide-orbit at the time. We can take big scientific survey ships, manned, to any of the planets or moons, do a thorough job of exploring and return to Earth. The round trip, allowing say, thirty days for the explorations, will take five weeks."

"But ... why would that be classified top secret?" Len asked, frowning. "We all profit from exploration of that kind! We could build the ship with everyone else and share the cost!"

"No way! The ship would be propelled by a series of very small hydrogen bombs, in effect. If we can build cannons that fire a shell – with a hydrogen bomb instead of powder – we can set off a hydrogen bomb of any size anywhere with a laser and some heavy hydrogen. You could almost carry the thing in your pocket and it would *not* be detectable."

"We could also set off any nuclear material in something like a missile in the atmosphere," Tony said. "It's only a matter of time.

"So let's get back to Ed and friend Auermond, shall we? We can prevent one murder, at least!"

"Guhhhh! Sheeee!" Len remarked.

<u>*Chapter eight*</u>

I went home for a nap. I would be up at twelve to be in on the fun things at Ed's place and wanted to be wide awake and fresh. We decided we couldn't very well know how to act toward Wilder until we saw how Auermond and friend would act. I expected them to call Wilder as soon as they reached Tampa, but Len didn't. He didn't think they'd call him long distance from anywhere simply because that would leave a record.

There was a surveillance of Wilder's place and we now knew he hadn't gone to Tampa as the voice on the phone said, so I figured he was expecting a call from Auermond and wouldn't answer any others.

I was back to the beginning of this case again, in a way. It all figured very well without Wilder, but it didn't make much sense with him. All of what we'd discussed fit well enough, but why he was in it from the first did *not* begin to fit. The case held perfectly from the point he entered the scene, but didn't give us any reason for him to have ever gotten involved. Even if the Israelis knew what the research project was about they would never have gotten involved in such a way before there was any progress – and probably not after.

I laid back in bed trying to find a starting point for it. It had to be before the research started, but after they found the building and began modification for the labs. That was obvious. It didn't lead to any why. If I didn't find the why I wouldn't ever know if the whole case was finished. I didn't need little things popping up later.

I finally drifted off thinking maybe Tony would come up with something and dreamed of JK and Auermond trying to get my funds from the bank. I kept trying to steer them toward simply writing a check for it, but JK was determined to do it with a computer while Auermond wanted to send the Israeli army after it. Tony was advising JK and Len was advising Auermond. Cal was arguing Dave was really behind it, trying to get the funds to build a huge platinum spaceship he'd call "The Maita" – while Dave wanted to go fishing, but couldn't use the boat because Jim and my wife were out in it. Paulo was dumping all the stud orchids, claiming we needed the room to grow our tomatoes in salt water. Lou had all the kids locked in the underground house because that way she would know they were safe when the Israeli army started shooting up the place getting my money – which she had hidden in the deep freeze.

Well, that made as much sense as the facts in the stupid case. Len and Tony might feel we had it all wrapped up except for the details, but I had a very bad feeling about it. I was afraid it would never be safe to do this kind of research if we didn't stop this kind of thing right now.

That was a very strange thing to suddenly be thinking! My weird subconscious knew something again! I was at that stage where I wasn't really awake and I wasn't quite asleep, either. I knew from experience my subconscious mind had made some kind of weird connection I hadn't consciously considered. It would be important to find out what it was. My trouble was that it would come in its own time. I couldn't call it up at will.

I got up about ten o'clock and had a good hot meal and some coffee, then drove to Len's house, where Cal was waiting for us. We talked about a few things until Tony drove up, then got into Len's car and the FHP cruiser Cal drove to head for Ed's house. Ed and JK were at the Crane plant in Sarasota playing with the computer lab.

I rode with Len while Tony rode with Cal. We pulled into an allnight cafe about three blocks from Ed's place. Len took his portable radio pickup in. It picked up the broadcast from his car set, which was on a special frequency from the FHP. We had been informed the plane had landed and Auermond and friend were in a rented car heading down the interstate. They should arrive in fifteen minutes or so. We got a call that they'd stopped at a Circle K a couple miles up the road to use the payphone.

"Um-hmm Calling Wilder," Len suggested. "I think we've got them figured pretty close."

Ten minutes later they were parked on the road behind Ed's house. I expected us to get up and head out, but everyone sat there, so I didn't say anything. Suddenly, Tony's pocket made a whining sound. "That's it! We have them!" he said and stood, so we all got up, though no one was in a big hurry. We paid the check and strolled out, drove to Ed's house and went in with a key Tony produced. He took out a little radio scanner unit from his pocket, looked at it, said, "Kitchenette," and went on back along the hall. The door to the kitchen was closed, so Tony opened it with an electronic cardkey. There was an open window in the little alcove – with bars across it. Auermond was sitting at the table.

"Very clever," he greeted. "Was it a trap all along or does that Vore guy use this kind of sec system all over this place?"

"Oh, Oi think we had it all figured, don't you know!" I said.

"That's damned hard to believe!" Auermond exclaimed. "I've never been fooled by a disguise before! I knew you were in London, but you fooled me!"

Len took his portable out of his pocket and asked, "You get 'em?"

"Roger! One female that we followed from Tampa."

Female? Auermond suddenly wasn't so cool.

"We've had you under constant surveillance since you arrived in Tampa," Cal said. "It's not going to be so easy this time."

Tony looked at a little panel screen in a dish cabinet by the alcove, opened the silverware drawer and searched through the cutlery there. He then looked puzzled and shrugged at Len.

I watched Auermond's eyes. He was much too watchful and seemed almost relieved when Tony closed the drawer. I could figure what happened.

"It's in there."

"The telltale says he didn't open anything except that drawer after the bars locked," Tony said. "There isn't anything added to the stuff there."

I grinned, slid the drawer all the way out of the cabinet and reached into the space behind and below the drawers, then stopped before I touched anything. I borrowed Cal's glove, then reached in to carefully remove the curved bronze knife with a large knobby handle there.

"This is good quality cabinetry," I said. "It isn't open under the drawers to the shelves below. There's a solid partition. It had to be there or taped to the back of the drawer."

"I'd say this is going to put you in the chair for the murders of Gus Eisingstein and Ralph Meiner," Len said.

"Eisingstein?" Cal asked. "I thought...."

"Gus was killed in that sealed vault with this knife," Len interrupted quickly. "Ralph Meiner was also killed with this knife and our friend here has possession of the knife. We have videos of this turkey leaving that vault with this knife in his hand! He's going to fry!"

"I refuse to speak more in any manner," Auermond announced, sharply. "I will claim diplomatic immunity and demand to speak with the Israeli Embassy!"

"You don't have any immunity, diplomatic or otherwise. You're a spy, not a damned sleazy diplomat!" I snapped. "If you'd presented a diplomatic passport at Tampa International I'd have shot you right between your damned eyes when we came in here – before you had any chance to identify yourself. Breaking and entering is a felony and I could have sworn I saw a pistol in your hand – *and* that knife!"

"There would have been an Uzi and a grenade when I came in here to investigate," Len agreed. "I don't play those damned idiotic international games, either. You aren't going to get away with coming here and killing American citizens and neither is anyone else! If we don't stop it now it'll only get worse."

Len read him his rights and we went en mass to the sheriff's department where the FHP people brought in a dark woman and said her passport said she was Ilya Voranov from Mansk.

"You have nothing you can hold Ilya on," Auermond said. "She will bring embassy people here to arrange for my release. Go, Ilya! They can't stop you!"

"Yeah, we can," Cal said. "She came across the Atlantic Ocean with you, drove a car from Tampa to here for you and was waiting to take you back. You'd committed a couple of murders and were here to commit another. She's what we call accessory to the fact, meaning she's as guilty as you are, legally."

"I don't think it's sunk in at all," Len said dryly. "You're under arrest for murder one and attempted murder. No embassy is going to have you released and neither is the state department. Israel isn't going to come to your aid because they simply can't afford the embarrassment and our state department isn't going to try to intercede because they learned a long time ago not to mess with Grimes. He can give them a lot more publicity than they want, what with these other spy things."

He leaned down and looked the seated Auermond straight in the eyes. "You're going to be strapped in the chair and an electric current is going to be passed through your body until you are dead, dead, dead!" he hissed through clenched teeth. "Get that fact through your thick stupid head. We have you seven ways from Sunday!"

"You might want to answer a few questions here," Cal suggested. "It could go easier on you. It will definitely go easier on the, er, excuse the expression, lady."

Auermond shut up and glared.

"Your choice!" Len said.

"I'm glad," I said. "I don't want any deals. I want him to fry and her to be eighty years old when she gets out."

"Cathy! Earl! Take this excrement out of here and put them in maximum security," Len called.

We waited until the two were led away.

"They're both deferring their phone calls until later in the morning when the embassy's open in Tampa," Len said.

"I'll contact their ambassadors through Crane before the place opens," Tony promised. "I think I can explain a few of the facts of life to them. They understand money like yours and power like Crane's."

"Their embassy doesn't want anything to do with them," Cal said. "I had some friends in Tallahassee get in touch with them when we knew they were coming here. They don't represent Israel in any way. They're breaking Israel's laws by doing this, as well as ours. They'll have to try to get Wilder to get them out – and there ain't no way, José!"

"Wilder! I forgot him!" Tony said, and picked up the phone. He talked for a minute to the night receptionist at Crane, then was connected with JK at the computer labs. They talked a few minutes before Tony suggested we go to Crane before we faced Wilder with anything. JK found some-thing.

We went to the Crane plant, where JK handed us about six pounds of computer printouts. I saw the "top secret" codes across the tops of some of them and raised an eyebrow at

Tony.

"Yup! JK can access the FBI, CIA, IRS, banks, The Yard, Interpol, the KGB and anything else on any computer links," Tony said. "All he has to do is find the code. He made a little machine that sits around finding access codes for us. It's a little invention the government wants to buy. His research now is finding ways to protect sensitive secret information from such intrusive little gizmos."

"It can't be done, I don't think," JK said. "If it's in the machines it can be gotten out of the machines. If the machine is on-link to anything the information is there for the taking."

"But that means they can get all our secrets!" Len cried.

"If you mean Russia, they've got ours and we've got theirs. I'm in constant communication with scientists in Russia who're doing the same general kind of research I'm doing. We trade lots of information."

"What the..?!" Len exploded. "Christ! That's giving them classified information!"

"No it isn't," Tony argued. "Our research doesn't exist in any formalized sense and neither does theirs. You can't classify research you aren't doing. It's just a few scientists talking to one another."

"I learned how to find what the plant CD asked me about in Texas was doing from Leo, a regular contact in a place called Cherdinsk," JK explained. "He even suggested we could...."

He got a faraway look in his eyes and wandered off toward the labs. Tony grinned and shrugged.

"JK won't give them anything and they won't give him anything. They simply verify each other's work.

"JK found a system that makes it really hard for them to find certain information – the really important stuff – for us. We're using it now. I imagine they're doing the same."

"Don't you think we should concentrate on our case?" I

asked.

"You'll have to do it without me," Cal said. "I'm on duty in an hour and I want to get home to change and tell Wilma I didn't skip entirely out of her life."

He left and each of the rest of us picked up a section of the stuff to read through. My part said Wilder's father's name was Eiderwilden. He was a German Jew who escaped before things got really bad, went to England, then came to the US a few months after the war ended. That explained a lot.

He was one of four kids. One brother had died of heart failure in '71, one sister was now living in Israel and one sister, the youngest of the family, was living in England.

Carson was the oldest, the next oldest was the sister, Sandra, who married a man named Abraham Solomon and moved to Israel with him in '76. The dead brother was David and, as I reached that part, I heard Tony whistle.

The youngest sister, Cleo, married Abraham's younger brother, Mortimer, who listed his present address as The Three Larches, Leepstead Under Hamilton, Hartfordshire, England, UK.

"Know who your lovely friend, Cleo, is?" Tony asked.

"Yeah. Youngest sister of Carson Wilder nee Eiderwilden," I replied. "I just thought of something my subconscious was trying to get across when I woke up this morning. Cleo looks a lot like Carson. If they were the same age they could almost be twins."

"It seems our case has become international, but not much like we first thought," Len said. "Auermond isn't anywhere in this part of it, but you'll never guess who Shartz is!"

"Family?" Tony asked.

"Mama's nephew. Mama was Helene Shartz. He's her kid brother's kid. This whole thing was some kind of crazy family operation!"

"Well, we can run over and ask Carson a few questions,"

Len said. "You're going to have to go back to England, aren't you?"

I thought about it. It seemed that would probably be the only way. I sighed, grimaced and nodded.

"Is Ilya part of the family?" I asked.

"I have the genealogy charts here somewhere," Tony answered. "Ah! Here!"

We waited while he read the list.

"No mention," he finally said. "Auermond isn't even a distant cousin."

We added what we intended to find from Wilder and got in Len's car. I wasn't sure we had anything to charge him with that would stick. A phone call from England wasn't enough.

"We'll just have to try to get him to say something," Len said. "The least we'll do is let him know he's not gonna get away with anything this time."

"I may be able to get enough to make a basic charge of accessory," I replied. "It'll be a matter of getting him to talk about a couple of things."

We found Wilder just waking up, ostensibly, but his eyes showed he hadn't gotten any sleep recently. He was short to the point of rudeness, to me particularly. After sparring around for a few minutes I sprang my own trap on him.

"Listen Wilder!" I snapped shortly. "We've been up all night arresting your two friends, Auermond and the lovely Ilya. I'm not in the mood to be diplomatic. I'm sure you're aware your money doesn't awe me in any way. Auermond called you from England, from the Airport Hotel, and had you gather information on where Ed Vore lives. You gave him that information when he called you from a payphone at a Circle K by the interstate a few hours ago. Len may want to try to trick you into saying something else, but that phone call ties you right squarely into the middle of an accessory charge you can't get out of!

"I'm tired! I want to go home and get a little sleep! Answer the damned questions and quit stalling around!"

"But I didn't have any idea why he wanted Mr. Vore's address!" Wilder cried, then looked like he'd been hit in the stomach.

"We already knew it. We want to know the rest of this. So help me, if anyone else is drawn into this or killed I'll see you fried! I mean it! The time for playing games is *over*, damn it!"

"You can't prove a damned thing! I'll answer nothing until I speak with my attorneys!"

"It's your decision to make," Len replied. "Don't, under any circumstances, try to leave the county or I'll let you cool your stupid ass in an isolation cell. I'm going to get three warrants charging you as accessory to two murders and one attempted murder, so you can start getting a really big wad of money together for your bail."

"Come on, guys. I want to get some sleep, too. I have to get the warrant signed, then we can all rest. I can send any flunky out here to pick him up."

We drove out with him glaring pure hatred at us.

"We got him on a minor accessory charge on the Vore attempted murder bit, but that's all," Len said. "I'll get a warrant and send a deputy out to put him in cuffs and ride him to jail in the back of the cruiser for all the neighbors to see. He'll be out before he's in, I guess. The lawyers'll be waiting at the station for us to bring him in.

"I think we really could all use a bit of rest. I'll have him picked up at two. We can spend a little time with our families or whatever. Fair enough?"

"Have him picked up at five, when all the neighbors will be home," I suggested. "The humiliation will soften him up a little, I suppose. He's very big on presenting a proper front among his snobbish friends out here. You really would be smart to keep a cruiser waiting outside of his gate here, though. He might decide to get out."

"I've already told the two I have working on surveillance to stick around and be conspicuous. I considered that," Len agreed.

I went home to work in the orchids, play with my kids and become reacquainted with my wife for a few minutes.

If we didn't get anything out of Auermond and his ladyfriend or Wilder I'd have to go back to England to try to get it out of Cleo, Shartz and Mort.

"Well, let's go on back to the substation," Len said, finishing his coffee at the Harde Luck Cafe. Cal had stopped to join us for a few minutes, then was going in to report, then go home. Len and I would try to get a little time to chat with Wilder before the lawyers corps descended on us. Claudette had called to say there were two waiting at the station for us to bring him in.

"We'll fool them!" Len said with a smirk. "We'll take him to the substation out at Myakka City. We can use the excuse that it's closest to the labs and to Ed's house, so it's where we'd naturally take him."

I grinned and we headed out. Len told the patrol to take the warrant, serve it and transport him to the Myakka substation. It would take the lawyers about half an hour to get there and would also mean they'd have to wait until we transported him back to Sarasota for a judge to set bail. There are many good, professional, reputable lawyers in Florida, despite the feeling one gets from seeing those ads the ambulance chasers have on TV. The ones waiting at the department were of the latter type, so we didn't much mind throwing every obstacle we could find in their way.

We were halfway to the substation when Len was called on the radio to be informed that one Carson Wilder had been discovered, when a deputy and her assistant went to serve an arrest warrant, murdered. He had been shot through the head. Len hit the lights and siren, spun and we headed for the island.

"Damn!" Len exploded after a couple of minutes. "We had the car watching the place the whole time!"

"We have the whole damned bay out there," I said. "They probably came by boat. What I don't understand is how the officer in the car *and* the maid failed to hear the shot.

"Nobody heard it, did they?"

"I don't think so, but why that strange connection with the officers and the maid?"

"Outside, the cops would hear it, but the maid might not, inside. Inside, the maid would hear it, but the cops might not."

We screamed into the drive and up to the house. We were both out of the cruiser before it had completely stopped rolling. The coroner, Slats Lattimer, was just taking his bag from his station wagon. He nodded curtly at me, greeted Len and went inside with us.

There was a sort of built-in lanai/conservatory in the center of the house with bromeliads, orchids, ferns, lilies and so forth planted or sitting around in pots. Wilder was slumped across a concrete bench.

"Inside. Maid," Len said.

I agreed and looked over Wilder's body. The bullet had gone clean through and hadn't expanded much. It was in the pecky cypress boarding to his left. I could plainly see the rip the bullet made hitting the board at an angle.

"High-powered rifle fired from about that doorway," I said. "A military rifle, probably. I'd say thirty-thirty or thirty-ought-six. Brass jacket slugs."

"Report, Dell, and don't elaborate," Len said to the deputy.

"We came as per our instructions to deliver a warrant and to arrest Carson Wilder. We were allowed inside by the housekeeper, Mrs. Connie Armundstedt, who said Mr. Wilder was in the plant room and led me here. She screamed when we discovered the body and fainted. My assistant put her on the sofa in the parlor area and called the department on the car radio while I stood watch here until the crime lab people arrived.

"You and Dr. Lattimer came immediately after the lab boys."

"Did you question the housekeeper in any way?" I asked.

"No. She had fainted. I didn't accompany Sal from this room. I have not left this room since I first entered."

"Good job!" Len said. "We know damned well nobody's touched anything.

"Sal! Come in here, will you?"

A deputy came in with a name tag saying "Salvatore A. Ginnini."

"Did you question the housekeeper yet?" Len asked.

"No, Sir! I'm in training and don't have the expertise."

"Very good! We don't allow our untrained personnel to question witnesses (to me) because, the way the courts are so damned anxious to let off any crook they can, the wrong kind of question at the wrong time can result in a mistrial – or worse.

"Get Mrs. Armundstedt.... No. We'll go in there. If she's gonna faint in here she won't do us any good."

Sal led us into the parlor, but no one was there. Len yelled for a search to be made and for her to be brought in as quickly as possible.

"They won't find her. She's gone," Len said.

"How do you figure?" I asked.

"If she was in this house when a thirty-thirty was fired she heard it. She would've come in here to investigate and would've found the body. Instead, she waits until the cops come in and leads them to the body, pulls the screaming wild faints and gets out as soon as she's alone. That car was in plain view all day out there, thus she knew she couldn't get out before. She had no way of knowing if the bay side was watched. That means she shot him. Period. No one else came into this house and no one left until the officers were occupied in here. She has about a fifteen minute head start on us.

"Dell!"

Della Norris, the deputy, came into the room.

"Yes?"

"Cars. Mrs. Armundstedt killed Wilder and used the time after you and Sal came in to make her getaway. Is there a car missing?"

She went outside and came back a few minutes later. "Brown nineteen eighty eight Toyota Celica two door sedan with silvered windows and one of those `Native' plates on the front. It was parked pointed out. I never saw the plate number. I'll call registration to see if there's anything registered in her name."

Len nodded and she went out. He first told her to put an APB to watch any cars that matched the description or to note any parked anywhere within six miles of the place, which was as far as she could have gotten in the time.

I called Tony to ask him if there was anything in our computer stuff about her and he said he'd put JK on it. We were to get in touch as soon as we had a license number or anything on that order for him to trace.

I was in what Wilder used as a study, so told Tony to hold on while I went through the little paper file marked "household" to pull out her file. I gave Tony her social security number and he said he'd get back in ten minutes with her entire life history.

Slats had the bullet out and said it was an old Enfield .303.

Great! England again!

Tony called back a couple minutes later. There was a conference speaker on the phone and Slats and Len were there, along with Sal and Dell. I turned the speaker on and said, "Give."

"George Harvey Matthews," Tony reported. "Wantaugh, Long Island, New York. Baker. Has emphysema. Drives a seventy nine Cadillac. Has about twenty thousand in the bank. Married. Owns his home and a ...."

"So the hell what!?" Len cried. "What's that all about?"

"CD gave me the social security and asked me to find out his entire history," Tony replied with a chuckle. "Sort of strange housekeeper. You think he was in drag?"

"Thanks, Tony," I said. "So she gave false credentials to get the job. Everything here is at a dead end except for Auermond and the lovely Ilya – and I don't think we're going to get a damned thing from them."

"She was planted here to keep a watchful eye on friend Wilder, apparently. This is a hell of a lot bigger than a couple of murders. A hell of a lot!"

I agreed. We talked a few minutes until Len's portable radio called him. I had Tony hang on.

"We located what appears to be the car described," a voice informed Len. "There is nothing registered in the name of Connie, Constance, C, or anything else that could be her. There is no car of that general type registered to anyone named Armundstedt in the state. There were two possibilities in cars found parked in shopping centers, so we ran a trace of the VIN numbers of both. One was stolen from Orlando, Florida, three months ago. It's now parked in Southland Mall, but there's almost no hope anyone saw anything there. There are thousands of cars on that lot."

"You hear that, Tony?" I asked.

"Yeah. Enough to know what they were saying. Maybe you can find some prints around that will trace back."

Len gave some instructions over the portable and held it in his hand, so I told Tony to hang on. A minute later Len was called again.

"Go ahead."

"There's an old British Enfield rifle in the back seat wrapped in rags," the voice said. "It seems to be ... yes. Confirmed from shells inside. It's a three oh three. We'll run the serial numbers through the computers."

"Did you touch those shells?" Len asked, through his teeth.

"Negative. Training instructs all evidence that may contain prints or residues be handled with gloves or tongs. The shell was ejected and picked up with tongs to be read."

"Very good! I want prints from those shells and from anything else in or around that car!"

He gave more instructions, then I told Tony that was all we had.

The lab manager came in to complain there wasn't a print on anything anywhere in the house, so far as they could find.

"Uh-huh. She killed him, then spent the afternoon removing every scrap of evidence in the place," Slats moaned. "He's been dead about four hours."

"She did the cooking. There's got to be a print on a pan or a glass or something. She sure as hell didn't clean every dish in this house in four hours."

Slats gave the lab crew new instructions. We all looked around some more and were about to head for Len's office when Slats came out to say he had a good set of prints that may be hers. "She didn't bother to wipe off the stuff in the garbage can. She opened a can of cat food this morning and we have almost her whole right hand on it. There's also a Taster's Choice coffee jar in there with the thumb and two fingers from her left hand."

Now and then we get a break. It would be great if these prints were on file somewhere!

Chapter nine

I worked in the orchid flasking room all morning, flasking some of my crosses. Alma could keep up with her own, but we each had our own method.

There was really nothing to do on the case until I heard from Len on the prints. If we were luckier than we ever are we could solve this thing without my having to go to England again. It would be mostly a matter of finding Connie Armundstedt. The prints were faxed for ID to Washington. Tony was in touch with the Israeli embassy in Tampa, who angrily declaimed any knowledge whatever of Auermond, Shartz or anyone else connected with the case. There was no department such as the one they claimed to represent to Gus Eisingstein. They were doing a thorough check to see if they were members of any of the radical groups in Israel, but believed they were probably from England, where there were a number of splinter extremist groups who blah, blah, blah.

Auermond's passport was legitimate and stated he was a citizen of Israel. Ilya's passport said she had been a Ukranian Jew who was now a citizen of Israel. Her passport was legitimate, too. Tony can check on that sort of thing. I'd be willing to bet JK could find the information before they could send out the disinformation from Israel. They weren't proud of those kinds over there anymore than we're proud of some of our own types. They would try to cover anything that could result in bad publicity. They'd had enough of that. In my opinion, they brought it every bit on themselves. They elected the ones who perpetrate those actions, just like we elect the ones who embarrass the US.

I went fishing with Jim in the afternoon, then Alma and I went to the Asolo Theater in Sarasota to see a delightful comedy. The critics had panned it terribly so we knew it would be good.

Next morning I spent in the orchids until the call came from Len.

"Her name is Carla Sohn. She was from Sweden, originally, but now has residence in Haifa. She's known to be connected with any number of radical movements. She's even wanted for questioning in Israel concerning the shooting of a local liberal politician and a bombing in the occupied territory. She's wanted in Lebanon for murder and is listed as a terrorist – believe it or not – by Syria, who has a price on her head.

"You met her. Dell and Sal said she was the `Aunt Lucy' type. Sweet and charming and very deferential."

"She seemed a rather normal pleasant and comfortable typical housekeeper the only time I met her. She's really Jewish?"

"Yup! Radical extreme Zionist. Eye for an eye and I get to you first so you can't hurt me. Pre-emptive strikes, I think they call them."

"I hit him because I thought he might hit me, so it's self-defense. Standard line.

"Any connections I should know about?"

"Stayed in London for three months a year and a half ago, but was asked to leave the country. She wasn't a citizen and was into the worst of the rabblerousers there," he answered and I groaned. It looked like I was on my way back to England.

"I take it you haven't found her yet?"

"She probably took a flight out of Tampa within hours of our little problem here. We think she went to Atlanta and they think she went to New York. I think she's on her way out of the country. It's far too obvious she killed Wilder. She can't hang around. I doubt she knows we found any way to trace her so we'll know the minute she tries to use her passport anywhere."

We talked awhile, then I went in to pack. Alma wanted to go along to visit our friends in England. Lou and Paulo said they'd take care of all the brats, so I was stuck with that. I didn't like to take my wife along on dangerous assignments, but that was settled.

Oh, well. Alma decided to first go to Milfordshire to see Sir Howard's collection and to visit with Lady Gwynne, then she'd go to Lancaster, then on and on. If I got through before she was finished with the tour I would join her. If not, we would meet again at the hotel.

No doubt I was going to take a planeload of orchids back.

I went to New Scotland Yard to meet with Sir William and Nigel and to catch everyone up to date on the case. Nigel pulled Carla Sohn's file, then called Interpol because there was a note saying there was a great deal about her in their files. The picture was of the maid I'd seen at Wilder's place. It was really her. I'd never doubted that because of the prints.

An agent came over with the information from Interpol. He was French and said she was wanted there as well as Belgium, Spain and Switzerland for terrorist activity. She was with a little group who sent letter bombs to various people in those countries. One person had already been killed by one of them and several others were seriously injured. She was, apparently, not a very nice lady.

The Yard file said she was mixed up with a group who had tried to get into politics in local areas. She was staying – you'll never guess – in a village called Leepstead Under Hamilton when she was asked to leave the country. It wasn't known until several days after she'd left that she was Carla Sohn and not Phyllis Solomon. Interpol had backtraced her when she used her passport in Canada, but she'd disappeared by then. This was the next place they heard of her.

"Claimed to be a relative of dear Mort?" I asked.

"Didn't claim anything. She'll let anyone assume anything they want. Doesn't get into as much trouble that way."

"I imagine she'll disappear again and Interpol will be left with egg on their faces again," Sir William said.

I was looking over the stuff the Interpol agent brought over and saw something. "How fast can you have someone looking for her in Toronto, Canada?" I asked.

"About fifteen minutes," the Interpol man said. "Do you see something?"

"I'm not sure, but it's worth a chance. She's known to have first entered Spain from Israel through Barcelona. She went from there to Switzerland and was with the radical group there, then went back to Barcelona, where she went to Paris. From Paris, she came to England and stayed until she was asked to leave, went back to Paris, then into Toronto. From Toronto she went down to Florida and got into trouble and she's thought to now be in New York.

"She seems to enter a country through a certain port, probably because she can get the phony ID there. She goes into another country, gets into trouble, then leaves through the same port she came in, probably because she uses her real passport as security when she gets the phony crap."

The Interpol man had the phone before I was through. He barked some orders, then turned to me, grinned, and said, "It's worth a betting chance. Barcelona and Paris could be simple coincidences and not a pattern, but if she's headed toward Toronto third time's *no* coincidence! It's probably just an unconscious pattern, but patterns are deadly in this game!"

He winked and left.

"Have you figured who and what is behind this?" Nigel asked. "It all seems a bit mad, what?"

"Crazy like a fox," I said. "I think there's a lot less to this than meets the eye."

"Less, yes," Sir William agreed. "It seemed to me you

were off finding all these things, one leading to another, and now the connection with the original problem is tenuous, at best. You started in Florida with a murder by a person in Florida. That murder was motivated by a simple desire of a person from a persecuted race to try to stop something that would add to his race's persecution and oppression. You solved that one very quickly. This Vore person did it – and, furthermore, I agree with him and would do the same!

"That first murder led to a second, but the connection was more on the order of secondary. Some international terrorists had infiltrated the laboratory and were planning to use their major discovery to blackmail the third world countries as well as the people whose oppression started the whole thing. Everything since is one big bloody attempt by everyone to cover his own ass! The fact is, you're involved with a ring of terrorists and spies now, like it or not! Bloody bad show!"

"I think it's probably more than that, but less than what we were thinking earlier. There's another person who was actually manipulating the whole deal all along. He was simply trying to get everyone involved to be exposed or to kill everyone else off. He was very damned successful, you know. He now has the terrorists killing each other off and the worst of them will be exposed. They can't hope to escape that.

"I just wonder if he knew all along about Carla Sohn. I wonder if he set this whole thing up to get to her, specifically, caught for some reason."

"He could get her by simply turning her in to Interpol!" Nigel exclaimed.

"I wonder. He's a Jordanian living in the US. I wonder if maybe he hasn't tried to finger her.

"Oh, hell! I wonder how he was able to get Wilder to insert himself into the whole mess! That's what started it!"

"I think you can keep an eye on Shartz here. Auermond may try to implicate him to make it easier on himself."

"Before you run off back to Florida and ruin your case there you can go about the country with your lovely wife to gather some orchids and think," Sir William suggested. "I think I know you well enough now to say you will ruin everything if you don't allow things to stand as your friend, Sheriff Stewart, has set them up."

"You've lost me. What has Len set up? How can I ruin anything?"

"Do as I say, then you and Alma will join Nigel and myself for dinner before you return stateside," Sir William suggested. "If it hasn't become obvious to you by then I'll explain how you may end up allowing Auermond to get away with murdering Ralph Meiner if you fail to consider the larger ramifications of precipitous actions or words."

When I went to find Alma I still hadn't quite figured what he meant.

The orchids were aboard and inspected, the plane was serviced and ready, our luggage was aboard and Alma and I were sitting at a table in the hotel restaurant across from Nigel and Sir William. Alma and I had spent eight more days visiting and buying or trading with those who would never sell a part of a particular plant (Much as Alma and myself), but who would swap a plant for another to a person who could really appreciate it. Stud plants all.

I wasn't sure what we were going to discuss, but I was ready. We finished the meal and moved to the terrace for brandy. When we were settled, Sir William asked if I had figured what he meant about the case being ruined.

"Not really. It has to do with Ed Vore?"

"You can't go in there and say he committed the first murder," Sir William warned. "If you do that Auermond will get away with killing Ralph Meiner. You must realize the killing of Gus Eisingstein really was justified. Completely.

Totally. Absolutely. He was acting as a traitor to the US, you see. That can't reasonably be denied. He was acting in a manner that made it necessary to stop him in defense of Mr. Vore's own family. That is justifiable homicide, even if the victim isn't a traitor."

"I think Gus Esingstein was probably only terribly misguided," Alma said. "CD told me about the case to see if I could understand why you thought he would ruin it. Gus was always manipulated into doing what he did."

"His personal motivation for being a traitor is secondary to the simple and obvious fact that he *was* a traitor!" Nigel insisted. "He may have been following the only right and pure course in his own mind, but he *was* a traitor. He *was* giving classified material to a foreign power. The main reason one must remain firm and wholly uncompassionate about this sort of situation is because of what actually was happening. He wasn't giving this material to any friendly power, even though I'm sure he believed wholeheartedly he was doing exactly that. He was passing it to a few international thugs and terrorists."

"I had already figured that. If I jump in and say Ed killed Gus Ed will admit it and that would mean the videos of Auermond with the knife in his hand won't mean diddly-squat. He could say he was taking the knife because it was a ritual blade and show the murder was committed by an anti-Israeli faction. He would when claim he was taking the knife into Vore's place to compare it to whatever he could find there because he was sure Ed Vore was the killer all along."

"But Ralph was killed with the knife while Auermond had it," Alma pointed out. "He can't get past that!"

"All we could prove is that Ralph was killed with a knife *like* that one. Auermond would serve thirty days for illegal entry into Ed's place."

"But ... but!" Alma stammered. "It's the same thing if Ed's

not charged with killing Gus! Auermond can argue all the same things!"

"If he's charged with killing Gus the videos of him with the knife in his hand and Ralph being killed with the same kind of knife can be tied together," Nigel said. "The fact he broke into Vore's place with the knife in his possession means he had the knife when Meiner was killed. There's no way he can untie the killings from one another.

"You see, if he can untie any one little thing the call to Wilder means nothing. With that tie-in it can be shown he was part of the gang who killed all of them – including Wilder. It destroys the gang internationally because we've finally found something the US will be unable to ignore."

"But it'll all fall apart because they would never kill Gus!" Alma cried. "He was working *for* them!"

"They kill their own people indiscriminately should question of their being able to harm the larger group be suspected," Nigel argued. "They would hesitate not one heartbeat to kill him if they felt they had what passes for a reason with such types."

"Such as Wilder," I reminded Alma.

"Yes. There's where Mr. Vore and his uncle are so very important to the whole rotten thing and must at all costs retain their credibility," Sir William said. "Kharavor will suddenly come forward to say he had faced Mr. Eisingstein with the truth about Auermond and Shartz. Mr. Eisingstein will have told him he was going to refuse the research data to them and was, in fact, going to turn them in to Israel himself, also explaining to Israel that he had already given them the tomatoes. Proof of what they were, you see."

"Therefore, Auermond killed Eisingstein to save his own worthless hide and to try to steal the research," Nigel continued. "Eisingstein had already given the research to Ed Vore for safekeeping, who gave it to Mrs. Seely in a surreptitious manner so as to not interfere in their investigation, which he felt would surely expose these international crooks if allowed to proceed naturally."

"But that's perjury!" Alma declared. "What tomatoes? I don't know what the hell you're talking about!"

I told her about the tomatoes the gang was holding that Gus had developed.

"I would applaud perjury, in this case," Sir William said. "It won't prove necessary, though. Auermond will plead guilty and throw himself on the mercy of the court in a useless attempt to protect the rest of the organization. They're all fanatics, you see. To deny killing Eisingstein would surely necessitate admitting to killing Meiner. He will opt for whatever protection the rest of the gang may be given by his keeping his mouth shut."

"But we had to do one other little thing," Nigel said.

"One other thing?" I asked. "I know the one little thing that's gonna make him squeal like a skewered pig. He can't protect anybody, now that we're after Carla. He would have to hope we never find her or there wouldn't be any point in sacrificing himself."

"We picked her up in Toronto one hour and eleven minutes after you told us she was heading there," Nigel said. "Now Interpol is holding her incommunicado. No one knows she was grabbed outside of this group."

"No. They'll definitely have had someone there watching her," I replied. "They'll know."

"Why, she went into the access tunnel to the plane immediately before it left Toronto," Sir William said innocently. "A woman fitting her description, who told the woman in the seat beside her her name was Carla, used her ticket and got off in Sydney, Australia, precisely as planned. She went into a restroom and never came out again."

"So her confederates will believe she knew Interpol was

hot after her and was getting close, so she disappeared on purpose!" Alma cried. "It's just like the books!"

"We sometimes do those things they write about, but it's not done nearly so spectacularly," Nigel said. "No car chases and parachuting into enemy territory to blow up the headquarters or anything. Simply make it all appear to be rather normal, under the circumstances.

"Sheriff Stewart reports Auermond was arraigned, as was Ilya Voranov. The trials will be in less than a month because they have insisted upon your speedy trial laws, then we're going to manage to `catch' Carla when she escapes her kidnappers."

"Kidnappers?" Alma and I said at the same time.

"Interpol is aware of what all of us are doing and knows how delicate this operation is. They want this ring caught to the last man and know Auermond is the key *only* if Carla isn't on the scene," Sir William explained. "Therefore, Carla won't be on the scene. She will believe she was kidnapped by a PLO unit and is later to be transported to Syria or maybe Lebanon, but an opportunity to escape will come up at the right time. She will run directly into the arms of Interpol, who will have been alerted by an agent of theirs who had infiltrated the PLO group. The opportunity for escape will be because those PLO agents found the Interpol agents were coming and escaped themselves. It will also be very interesting to see which nest of hornets we stir with her kidnapping and who seems to be perhaps a bit overly interested. I also want to observe how a certain party in Leepstead Under Hamilton reacts, personally, in particular to the fact that she was then apparently in hiding with a PLO gang."

"I want to talk with a certain party in Gainesville. I think we can trade some very interesting stories!" We talked for more than three more hours, then Alma and I headed home.

There wasn't much more to do on the case, so I waited for the trials of Ilya and Auermond to do anything else. I was to be an expert state's witness in their trials, so could see exactly how closely Sir William and Nigel had figured Auermond. We were sitting at the prosecutor's table with everything we might need. I hadn't been told about much of the evidence, but that was only proper. Norton Miller, the prosecutor, was young and anxious and he seemed almost smug as the charges were being read.

"He's going to try to divide the cases," Nort whispered to me. "He'll claim he didn't have any reason to kill Gus, so the whole thing is ridiculous. He'll try to say he's working for Israel as a special agent and Gus was going to give them the research, so the idea of him killing Gus is purely unbelievable, therefore, he was equally innocent of killing anyone else.

"Boy! Is *he* gonna get a shock! He's gonna get it in my opening statement! He's gonna sit there knowing I've got him by the short hairs! He's gonna know he's heading straight for the chair!"

I wondered what he had, but kept my mouth shut.

There were about two hours of motions and attempts at a deal, which Nort turned down. I wasn't sure he shouldn't take a guilty plea of murder two for a twenty year sentence and drop charges against Ilya, but Nort laughed out loud and slapped the defense attorney on the back, saying, "The chair, Buddy! All the way! No deals!" just loud enough for Auermond to hear. Auermond sneered and looked smug, himself.

Judge Levitz asked if there was any opening statement. Nort said there was and stood.

"Ladies and gentlemen of the jury, this is a complex case, on the surface, but is really very simple, underneath. It's a case of an international spy and some terrorists, a scam and a man who was tricked into becoming a traitor.

"The state will show that the defendant did earlier receive a secret research tomato plant when he promised the world would benefit from the data and that Mr. Eisingstein's beloved Israel would benefit more than others when it was shown that they would give such an important thing to even their enemies! It would be to the good of all!

"When Mr. Eisingstein gave that data, that plant and those few seeds, some simple little tomato seeds, to Mr. Auermond, an agent for a foreign power, *in Mr. Eisenstein's certain knowledge,* he became a traitor to this country. Period! He stands convicted by his acts!

"The defense will try to make you believe he was only doing what he thought was best for everyone – *and that is true*! What they will try to overlook is that he wasn't dealing with any such humanitarian organization, he was dealing with known terrorists who would use that research as a weapon.

"I have affidavits here from New Scotland Yard in England and from Interpol explaining much about this group the defendant so proudly counts himself a member of. My correspondent with New Scotland Yard points out that the laws against disseminating this research simply must be enforced without regard to the intent of the act *because* such a situation as *this very one* may occur.

"A plant capable of being watered with sea water that produces quality food for a starving people is still being suppressed *and is a weapon against those very people*!

"Next they will say Mr. Eisginstein was going to give them the new research. That is why they were *there*!

"That is not true. The state will prove how the facts of how the tomatoes were used was made known to Mr. Eisingstein and that not only was Mr. Eisingstein not going to give them the research, he *and Mr. Ralph Meiner*, with aid of another party were going to turn Mr. Auermond and a Mr. Shartz over to the FBI and Interpol as spies and international thieves and terrorists!

"We will prove also that both Mr. Auermond and Mr. Shartz are wanted for terrorist activity in France and Spain, among several notable others in this organization he is so proud of. We will prove they are connected to a gang of thugs and terrorists in England.

"We will prove that a Mr. Carson Wilder was their contact man here in Florida for the terrorist group and that, because Mr. Wilder knew too much, he also was subsequently *murdered* by the group.

"We have solid evidence from Interpol that his murderer is a woman known to them as Carla Sohn. She is being sought at this time. Interpol records indicate she is wanted in various countries for bombings, thievery and several other killings.

"We will show you security video tapes of this same Mr. Auermond and Mr. Shartz exiting a security lab vault in which the first victim, Gus Eisingstein, was found stabbed to death. Those videos will also show beyond any possible doubt that *no one* entered that vault after that time until the body was found.

"We will point out in those same videos that Auermond has the murder weapon *in his own hands* as he left that vault where the mutilated body of Gus Eisingstein was found. We will prove that Ralph Meiner was killed with that same knife, that traces of blood of his type *and his rare prescription medicine* were discovered in the haft guard of that knife.

"We will prove beyond any doubt whatever that Mr. Auermond broke into the home of Eduard Vore in an attempt to make him the next victim and that he brought *that very knife* with him. *That* is where we gained possession of the murder weapon!

"We will show that all of this came about because Mr. Auermond is a fanatic who puts an idea proved false by all of recorded history and condemned by every other country in this world ahead of everything decent in life. We will find the rest of this gang of thugs and we will bring them to justice!

"The prosecution will ask, nay, we will *demand* – the prosecution will *demand* death in the electric chair for this most foul, heinous, coldblooded, fanatic murderer!

"Thank you, Your Honor, ladies and gentlemen."

"Does defense wish to make a statement at this time?" Judge Levitz asked.

"Your honor, I wish to state here ... what?" Auermond's lawyer began. Auermond pulled at his sleeve and whispered into his ear. They argued for a moment until Judge Levitz said, "Counselor, we're waiting!"

"Er, I, that is...." the lawyer stammered. "A moment, your honor. My client wishes to change his plea. I feel that would be ill-advised."

"I can take a five minute recess for you to consult," Judge Levitz said, and banged her gavel.

The bailiff handed her a sheaf of papers and she began signing writs and other things. She looked up after five minutes, banged the gavel and said, "Court is still in session. Counselor?"

"Defense attorney hereby withdraws from the case on insistence of the client. Request postponement of trial until such time as other representation is secured."

"Denied!" Levitz snapped. "That's a ploy that might work on TV or in some minor fender-bender, but it won't work here. There has been ample time to prepare the case and defendant agreed to this date and this time for trial. Defendant, in fact, insisted upon early trial.

"Court also refuses dismissal of attorneys on either side."

"Defense will remain under duress and as advisory only. Defendant claims preparedness to enter his own plea and to conduct any defense as he sees fit."

"Does defense have an opening statement?" Levitz asked of Auermond.

Auermond stood, smirked and answered, "Plea of nolo contendre to all charges."

"You realize that is a guilty plea?" Levitz asked.

"Nolo contendre," Auermond said and sat. Nort smirked at me.

"If it comes to trial we'll bring others of the gang into it. He doesn't know if we have anything. This will keep him from letting the cat out of the bag. When he saw we knew Eisingstein was preparing to turn him down and report him, he was going to fight us for a second degree, but we would bring the espionage angle into it so that would be risky. When he saw we knew who killed Wilder and why he had to look at the possibility we would catch her and his testimony here would inevitably tie her into it – if we knew anything.

"Slats Lattimer really came through with that knife. Type O negative might be as common as all hell, but levo-diprozartamine valearate is one hell of a rare medication. Right there he knew we could beat anything he could pull. If we could positively connect that knife with Meiner we had him!

"We did it!"

"I never heard of that compound," I said. "What is it?"

"It's a medicine that stops precancerous cells," Nort said. "It's experimental, and there are only sixty people in the entire state who are taking it in a test. Meiner had two precancerous polyps removed from his throat about three months ago and is the one person in this area of Florida who had any access whatsoever to the stuff. Now we can get this Voranov woman on accessory charges easily enough. Interpol is interested in her, too, so we may want to extradite her. I've refused extradition for Auermond. Levitz will give him life without possibility of parole on both murders. He'll be held in maximum security.

"I think now we'll dig up more on him. He may be tried in a couple of other places on capital charges. Before it's over he's going to either be gassed or electrocuted.

"Did you know Israel said they don't want anything to do with him and even said they'd send his records to court, along with official disclaimer? He's wanted for questioning there, too!

"Wow! An international trial – and it's only my third case!"

I almost reacted, but I saw what Len had done there. This one didn't know his way around enough yet to make a deal. He wanted a reputation and he would be more likely to accept the affidavits from Kharavor and would work with Nigel without question, where a more experienced lawyer would be asking all kinds of probing questions and wouldn't trust a bit of that. He would start digging on his own and might find a thing or two to make him back off.

Len was standing in the hall as I left so we drove over to the Harde Luck Café for coffee and talk.

"I don't think I would have gone through with this if Slats hadn't found that medication. It was barely possible until that time that someone like Sohn had actually killed Ralph and Auermond was merely stonewalling to give them time to escape. That stuff put it smack in his hands.

"Your friend, Lord William, is smart as all hell, isn't he?"

"It's Sir William. What did he do?"

"He told me to arrange for a young and inexperienced prosecutor who wouldn't ask a lot of questions, give him all the crap, make a few slight suggestions and let him run with it. He said statements like the ones from Kharavor, statements that wouldn't hold up for two seconds, should be alluded to in the opening statement, along with a lot of facts they didn't know we had before that minute and Auermond would plead guilty. He said it would be a `no contest' plea, which is as good. Auermond can't appeal that plea!"

I saw what that was about. In most parts of Europe Auermond could later claim duress, but in the US it was the same as a guilty plea. He couldn't appeal it because he'd had advice of counsel and had ignored it.

Now we could bring out Carla Sohn and try to clean the rest of this mess up.

Chapter ten

"You have the right to be in on this," Nigel answered. "You're the one who got the whole thing rolling. We have to extradite her here to England, but that's already arranged."

"I'll fly over. I can bring the stuff Alma and I traded for rather than shipping it over commercial. I'll call Sir William and he can have the customs and agriculture inspectors ready. I got the exchange permits when we left. I seem to spend at least half my time flying back and forth across the Atlantic lately!"

"It's a good thing you're so wealthy! Nobody else could afford one of your cases."

We talked awhile longer, then I called Sir William, made the arrangements and went out to the greenhouses to tell Alma about it. She grinned and said she'd be glad when I finished with this silly damned case so my kids could spend enough time with me to at least know my name was "Daddy!"

Lou and Paulo had taken care of ours while we were in England before, so they'd take a vacation when I was back and we'd take care of theirs. I still think all those kids are going to be confused as to exactly which of us are their parents! Lou and Paulo (And Alma) speak Spanish about half the time when the kids are around, so they all speak Spanish and English, both without accent. Shirley Bock has them speaking German, as well. I can understand a little Spanish ... who cares?

I took all the plants Alma had set aside for the trades, boxed them and labeled what they were and who they were for. It was going to take about four days for Carla to be extradited, so I'd have time to deliver all of them. I wondered if I should stop at Gainesville to talk with Yusef Kharavor, but decided to wait. I knew most of his part in this, but I did want to know how he was able to pull it off. I would make the flight directly to London.

Jim and I took the bay boat out and got some clams and shrimp, then went to a barrier island and gathered coquinas, then caught a mess of sheepshead for dinner. I would leave in the morning.

"I think this Screaming Feather is as good as the FCC and better than the one we used for a parent on Falcon Feather," I told Sir Howard. "The gold tracings are very distinct. Alma said to tell you it hasn't been judged because she put a pod on her division of it, then never got around to it. If it isn't satisfactory we'll make it up."

"Satisfactory?! Humpfh! I just asked for a good Screaming bloody Feather! If I trade very often with that woman I'll become famous for my collection! That cross of my Malvern on Golden Coin is going to be nice. Take her a dozen seedlings to make up a part of the difference. Take the piece of Golden Coin I used as a parent."

He insisted, so I was going to have to take another load of plants back with me.

I called on the rest of the people we owed plants to and most of them said we'd cheated ourselves and made me take more plants back "To even it up a bit." I bought a nice new collection of dendrobes from an estate several local collectors told me about. Might as well make a load of it!

I stayed at the hotel where I'd stayed both times before so I could dine with Sir William. He was an excellent host and showed me around London. It's a fascinating city.

Nigel called on my third night there to say Carla would be in and through the paperwork the following afternoon. I could be in the listening room when she was interrogated.

"CD? Nigel here," greeted me when I answered the phone

before daylight.

"Uh-oh!" I answered.

"She was murdered right there in Heathrow! We were being so very careful! We brought her in on a special plane Interpol supplied and even brought her in through a gate way off to the side that's hardly ever used! I can see how they would figure we'd do that, but I don't know how they got the bomb in there."

"I'm on my way. Wake Sir William and tell him to meet me in the lobby in five minutes." I jumped out of bed, dressed as fast as I could and headed for the lobby. Sir William got there about three minutes later and we jumped into my rented car to head for Heathrow Airport. Sir William spotted a police cruiser and had me blow the horn so he could wave to them. We stopped, he showed them his Scotland Yard ID and said to get us to Heathrow half an hour ago. We got there fast with the police escort.

Traffic was tied up tight around the airport while the police checked everyone going out. We went across a parking lot and to one end of the place, where I parked near the wad of police and ambulance vehicles. Sir William trotted on in, but I stopped to look over the area outside. I noted all the cars still there, then went on in. Nigel saw me and waved for me to come over.

"They placed the bomb in a trash receptacle," he reported. "Small plastic thing, apparently. It used a radio set-off. They walked by it and someone pushed a button. Carla Sohn, Interpol Agent Andre Marquand and our own Chief Inspector George Potts died.

"I'm going to get them, CD. I promise you that. I'm going to get them! Damned good man, Potts. Wife and kid. I'm going to get them!"

"It was Shartz or the Solomons or both. The BMW's out there. I'm sure it's the same one Auermond had at their place."

"Cleo drove it in yesterday morning and took the early flight to Dublin. She hasn't returned. We checked on it *very* carefully. We know full well it was them, but we'll play seven bloody hells proving it!"

"Have someone check on exactly how valid that trip to Ireland was. This is how they got the bomb in."

"This lot is valet parking," Sir William said. "Find who came with her. Find the man who parked the car for her."

"Get the keys," I requested. "I want to look over that car.

"Look, Nigel. If I get out of line, tell me to shut up and mind my business. I'm aware I have no authority here, but I'm used to working with the police at home and admit to going too far a lot of the time."

"I'm willing to let you run with this a bit, but only to a point. You're obviously used to giving orders. It's part of being a corporate mogul. I'll go along where it suits me. Fair enough?

"Now, as to the automobile! We have cause."

Nigel called a man over to give him a few instructions. The officer returned a few minutes later with a man in his early twenties.

"Roland Seaton," the officer said, handed Nigel a set of keys and went back to his watch.

"You parked the Solomon car?" Nigel asked.

"The blue BMW? Yeah, er, yes Sir! The lady was sort of weirdish, you know? Like spaced. Took her little hand valise and that huge ugly pocketbook – looked like a burlap sack, you know? Coke head. Real spaced, you know?"

"She was the only one in the car?" Nigel asked.

"Yeah. Spaced. Coke head. Real, like, sad. Looker if there ever was one."

Nigel nodded and said he could go back to his duties and we went to the car. Sir William looked in all the windows and tested all the doors to be sure they were locked.

"Lock when you push the bloody button. Can't tell if anyone was in there after the punkie left it here."

"There's nothing for anyone to hide under in the back, so there was no one in there," Nigel said. "If anyone was in the boot it would have been ajar. I know they check that here because there have been lawsuits when things were stolen."

I asked for the keys and opened the trunk. Everything seemed normal enough. There was plenty of room for a person to hide in there. I lifted the mat at the corners and drew out the wires to the electric trunk release. One of them was frayed. I very quickly searched around the wiring and found a piece not connected to anything. It traced back and up to the dome light wire.

I asked Sir William to open the front door, which he did. The lights under the dash came on, but the right dome light didn't. He checked and said there was no bulb.

I snapped the trunk lock shut with a screwdriver and touched the loose wire to the frayed spot on the trunk release wire. It snapped open.

I went to the door dome switch, unscrewed the panel behind it and pointed to the hot wire connected to the hot side of the dome light switch.

"Simple," Nigel said. "Kind of thing no one would think of. So our bomber and his bomb came inside the boot. The car was parked here, he waited a certain few minutes, then carefully opened the boot, slid out low so he wouldn't be spotted, went along the row of automobiles to the pedestrian walk and went in through the side door."

"So he's still right here or he's on the road out. He'll be stopped! He can't escape!" Sir William cried.

"Is there a flight to Dublin anytime soon?" I asked.

Nigel called the officer over as soon as we were inside and sent him off with instructions. He returned about ten minutes later. "There was one flight about twenty minutes ago and there will be one in eight more minutes," he reported. He gave me the flight numbers and terminals.

"I'll have someone waiting when the plane lands," Nigel said. "If either Shartz or Solomon get off of it they'll be taken into custody. Come on!"

We went to the boarding area for the next flight, went aboard to see no one yet on the plane, then checked the passenger list. Solomon was booked.

We waited until the plane was loaded, but Mort didn't show. Nigel asked the boarding attendant, who said "M. Solomon" never confirmed the reservation. That was what the little star was for – so his seat could be given to standby if he didn't show by five minutes to departure. We checked the list for the previous flight, which had "M. Solomon" with a star, but there was a line through the name.

"What does that mean?" Nigel asked.

"What? Oh! That cross-off there? He showed up before the five minute rule was up and boarded. He had never bothered to confirm the flight. Bloody nuisance! I say it should be ten minutes. They'd call and confirm it all then if they were going to be last minute!"

Nigel checked all the lists and found "M. Solomon" was booked on all flights since the previous night and was booked on the rest of them for today. There were a total of six more flights.

"Hang around here, set off your cute little bomb, fly out on whichever flight is next and come home with the wifey like you were with her the entire time she was in Dublin!" Sir William said. "What if we checked to be sure he was there all along?"

"I'm quite certain someone who would closely fit his general description was booked in some out-of-the-way inn or something and she met him there earlier," Nigel said. "They think of *almost* everything!"

"They bloody well didn't think we'd have who would find that boot trick!" Sir William said. "They didn't think we'd ever find the multiple bookings, either!

"Well, we have Solomon and Cleo. She's included all along as accessory and her meeting him there when he came in the boot of the car is our proof. They conspired to commit terrorist acts. Now it's to us to get that Shartz bastard. That should clean up the lot of them!"

"Good show! We'll meet the Interpol man back at the Yard," Nigel suggested. "He's bringing the entire dossier on Carla Sohn, Ilya, Auermond, Shartz and anyone else they've been known to work with. Let's finish this here. The plane lands in Dublin any minute and I want to be back at the Yard when they call in."

"I'd like to see the bloody damned bastard's face when they grab him!" Sir William said.

"Oh, they're going to return them here for questioning," Nigel replied. "He'll feel safe. He won't have any idea we figured how they did it. I think this is really all of the gang on this end. I think they're reduced to figuring out their own schemes. This wasn't nearly so professionally done as the things in the past when they had Carla to make plans and they had the contacts with the real heads of it in Israel.

"You see, they dare not contact anyone now. They're on their own."

"We have to make them implicate Shartz," I warned. "Right now, he stands a good chance of not being touched. We don't have enough solid evidence against him for any charge to be launched."

"... Herman David Shartz is a pyrotechnic expert specializing in plastic explosives and breaking safes to steal artwork and jewelry – which is why Interpol is on the case," M. LeDuc of Interpol said, handing Nigel the dossier. "We have proof he produced the items Carla Sohn used in the letter bombs. It's quite certain he made the explosives Sohn used to steal the Broadminton Diamond and some other things."

"Hmm. Specialty in radio fuses," Nigel stated, reading the comp paper. "He's good at wiring the letter bombs to the flap with a thin braided carbon steel wire. If they're cut open instead of unwrapped they still go off. Great with shaped charges."

"Good! Did the laboratory boys find any special fusing material?" Sir William asked.

Nigel called for a report and read on until it came in. He looked over the report and shook his head.

"The fact this was a plastic explosive, he's staying there and the Solomons used it is enough to get a warrant to search the house and grounds, isn't it?" I asked.

"The fact the Solomons used the thing is enough," Sir William agreed. "It's their house and grounds. Problem is, there won't be any evidence of anything at all there."

"I think maybe the evidence is right here in London," I suggested. "Remember; Shartz was going to go to the US with Auermond to kill Vore, but he changed his plans and sent the lovely Ilya instead. Think about that! They knew they would have to kill Wilder to shut him up if anything happened to Vore. Carla was there, so she was used. That meant Carla would skip back through Canada and would need some new little bombs for her next assignment. The Florida thing was just to keep her out of sight until the search for her had cooled down to where she wasn't such a priority. It was nothing like her regular specialty.

"Mr. LeDuc, who do they meet here in London?"

"Yes! We had them followed every inch in London!" Sir William exclaimed.

Nigel called for the reports on their movements from the moment they left Three Larches. M. LeDuc looked through his reports. The two officers suddenly cried, "Overberg Haberdashery!" at the same instant.

"We have wondered if Overberg was contact point," LeDuc said. "Several suspicious types seem to always drop in on him when in London, then safes get cracked and things stolen that show up in other countries."

"Is there a way we can get into his office or shop or whatever for a complete search?"

"What will we find?" LeDuc asked.

"Materials for building the bombs, at the very least. Shartz was going back into production of the letter bombs and got his supplies in hand. He suddenly put those supplies to use for another purpose."

"I would agree," Sir William said. "M. LeDuc has come from Interpol with evidence that links Mr. Overberg with terrorists, so we will search his commercial properties for further evidence on warrant of probability."

"Right!" Nigel snapped and grabbed the phone.

"This is an outrage!" Si Overberg yelled. He was a short, fat, very Jewish (Deliberately so) man with a high whiny voice. "Just because someone buys a hat or two from me and is later found to be a criminal is no reason to disturb my business!"

"No, but when every damned terrorist who ever comes to London comes in and none of them buy hats – that's reason!" Sir William retorted. "If you have nothing to hide here why get all hot and bothered because we're here??"

"It wrecks my business for all these police to be here. I have a sick wife and a kid who needs braces! I can't afford this disruption! I'll call my MP! You'll be sorry! Why are you doing this? You're anti-semites! That's it!"

"My name's Birnbaum and I didn't get this honker being anti-semite, you ridiculous ass!" Nigel spat at him. "My god!

There's nobody in London who looks more totally Jew than I do! What kind of accusation is that?! Shut up or I'll take you in for twelve hours of questioning on general principles!"

The team searched the place minutely, but didn't find anything amiss. I was ready to give it up when Nigel sent an agent to the Board of Architecture or something of the sort. The man returned with a set of plans for the entire block. It was pretty obvious without even measuring.

"Are you going to show us the entrance or do we tear the whole bloody wall down?" Sir William said. Overberg glared defiance and plopped down at his desk.

Sir William called two agents over and told them to throw the rows of hats on the shelves into the big trash receptacle in the rear alley. He picked up one fancy box, crushed it and threw it in the waste bin by Overberg's desk. Overberg squealed and actually began to weep big tears, crying that his whole life was being wiped out and that the hats were all he had in the world.

Sir William told the agents to get axes from the boot of his car and chop the damned wall down, hats and all.

Overberg showed us the entrance. It was behind a wide fulllength mirror. There were automatic weapons, various explosives, a very modern laser printing arrangement with a photo developer and stacks of phony unfilled passports from various countries. There was also money from other countries in boxes. There was anything anyone needed to establish a false identity. The Yard crew took everything in, along with Si Overberg. Nigel matched some of the packaging of the plastic explosives with a scrap found at Heathrow.

"We've still got everything but Shartz," Sir William noted. "The bloody damned bastard can't be tied to this well enough to convince a judge and jury if he has a barrister worth a damn!"

"So we'll get Cy Overberg to rat on him," I suggested.

"I agree," LeDuc said. "We have a good lever with that one."

"It's all an act with him," Nigel agreed. "He's as hard a customer as you'll ever see."

"Ah! Except for one small thing, I might agree!" LeDuc cried. "Here's what we'll do...."

"This is only a little chat," Nigel said to Overberg. We were, LeDuc, Nigel, Sir William, Overberg and myself, sitting around a conference table. "You can make your own choices, but all we want is one name, and we know that name."

"Kiss off!" Overberg snarled.

"I'm a special police expert from the states," I warned. "I think you'd better be very careful about offending any of us in this room any more than you have. Conspirators get the chair in the US and you're on your way there, buddy boy!"

"France, Belgium, and Switzerland want a crack at him first," LeDuc added. "Spain may add to that list.

"I'll lay this out so even you can understand it.

"There was a small bit of material found at the recent bombing at Heathrow. It was plastic explosive wrapping material. It's quite a common thing to find after those things. As a matter of fact, it was also found in all of those other places I mentioned after bombings.

"Now, we know Shartz made all the bombs for your friends Carla and Ilya, but it was *your* prints found on them. Carla's dead and Ilya's in detention, stateside. Only Shartz is here where we can tag him for this, but we can't tag him with the evidence we have.

"He got the stuff from you! It has *your* prints on it! Most of it was sent through the post and the others didn't handle the stuff without gloves. We didn't have a file match-up until we took yours today or you'd already be hanged!

"If you don't give us Shartz you get charged with all the bombings. Shartz will never be effective again, anyhow, and we may be able to get him in a situation where we can simply shoot him and end that little problem.

"We can tie you to every one of those bombings. We can't tie him to them without your evidence, so you take the fall. Refuse the Chief Inspector here and all you'll get is a little slap on the wrist for a couple of years. Refuse me and you'll be charged in five or six countries, then I'll turn you over to the Yank here. After about three years of constant trials you'll end up in their electric chair. Tell us nothing more than the truth. Tell us Shartz got those explosives and we'll let the Chief Inspector have you. Refuse and.... I trust you understand me, mon ami?"

Overberg glared at him and kept his mouth shut.

"Our Mr. LeDuc greatly underestimates me." I sneered. "I have no intention whatever of waiting or going to all that trouble and expense. I have other work to do and I'm not *officially* on this at all.

"You Zionist radicals have taught me well. I know what you do to the Palestinians and Jordanians. I'll make it plain you're an important part of that back home, then forget about you. There are plenty of Palestinians there who're anxious to wipe out your entire family to the last tenth cousin, including your kids who need braces and your sick wife. Personally, I hope you'll keep your stupid damned mouth clamped tightly shut. You'll eventually get to the US and will get the chair. We'll get everything we need from others, won't we, Sir William? It's already garnered a couple of witnesses' signatures?"

"Well, yes. We have those two people people coming in on a flight in a couple of hours from Dublin," Sir William answered.

Nigel called a warden to lead Overberg out.

"He'll break," LeDuc suggested. "If he thinks we'll take him out of England where he already has a defense prepared – bet the house on that – he'll do whatever he can to stay here. Anything we get from the Solomons will be gravy."

"We can work on them. Maybe we can make a deal where-under we let Cleo off if they give us Shartz," Nigel suggested.

Suddenly something said to me weeks ago fell into place! I laughed and said, "I think that would be a very bad mistake. Very bad, indeed!"

Cleo and Mort were led into the room shortly after eight the next morning. They had been brought in at a small airport not far from London and transported by car to New Scotland Yard to avoid any repeats of the bombing if we had missed anyone in the gang. There was twenty four hour surveillance of The Three Larches to ensure Shartz didn't get off the grounds. Nigel, LeDuc, Sir William and I sat around the same table we shared with Overberg the day before. I had eaten dinner with our little group the evening before, where we made the final part of our plan.

Cleo played the spacehead to perfection, but there was no way she could be that stupid and do the things she did.

Sir William and I let LeDuc and Nigel question them and act more and more frustrated by their answers – maybe a little *too* frustrated and just a little phony. Sir William waited until we saw the questioning look Cleo gave Mort and the slight nod she got in return. That was our cue that they had figured we knew something and were putting on an act.

"I say! This rot has gone quite far enough!" Sir William suddenly exploded. "They raather obviously will do and say only exactly what they must! Overberg's statement will put them behind bars! We're bloody well wasting time!"

"Now, let's not get off on some wild tangent!" LeDuc exclaimed shortly, while giving Nigel a pleading look. "I'm certain these people understand why we want information about, er, others who may have motive...."

"Crap!" I snorted. "Listen, you two phony idiots! I'm not an English cop and I'm not under the same restraints they are. I've wasted about enough time on this, already.

"We have everything! We've made a film of how the trunk was rigged. We've placed Mort in the airport to set the damned bomb off and we have Cleo as accessory, having driven him there and having tried to establish that stupid phony damned alibi in Dublin! We have the plane he boarded and his name on all the lists so as to be able to get himself out of Heathrow as soon as the bomb was used. We have those fingerprints on the bomb wrappings and all that testimony of Overberg. We have that secret arms room at his haberdashery. We have all those illegal weapons and supplies. We have Shartz manufacturing the bombs and we have you two using them. We have Shartz dropping the whole damned thing on you and Overberg's testimony to hang you!"

I turned to Nigel. "They're not going to tell you anything about the others because they don't know anything!"

"Shartz is trying to say...!" Mort cried.

"He can't say anything about us at all, Mortie dear!" Cleo quickly interjected. "I went to Dublin and met Mortie there later before we came back. There's no law against that. I have no idea what you found in any trunk."

"Trunk in Yank is the thing we call the boot of an automobile here," Nigel said defeatedly. "We found the hotwire to the dome light and the removed insulation spot on the positive wire to the release mechanism in minutes, of course.

"Mr. Grimes, we will probably learn a great deal more if you will refrain from informing the accused of our knowledge. You've told them much of what we have. That was not wise. Should you do any such ill-considered thing again I shall be forced to order you beingremoved from these proceedings!"

I sat back and mumbled.

Sir William said, "We have them. If Shartz wants to throw it all on them, so be it. We have a continuing watch on him that will hang him no matter what. Overberg's testimony about those plastic explosives, the fact he was observed picking it up – I bloody well agree with Mr. Grimes! If they want to protect Shartz, so what?"

"We don't care about Shartz," Nigel said. "We have all of that done and ready."

"What we need is to know the others in the gang," LeDuc said.

"That's easy!" I said. "Let them go home on bail. Hint that they're going to confirm Overberg's testimony and catch the rest of the gang when they come after them. They've proved they don't care if they kill each other off. Mort, Cleo and Shartz didn't let knocking Carla off bother them. Catch the others *after* they knock these two off and save the nation the expense of a long trial. You might even let Overberg go and don't even pick Shartz up. Observe, then you'll only have to prosecute the ones who knock these two off. Save a hell of a lot of money that way!"

"Bloody good show, CD!" Sir William cried. "All this bloody international intrigue is a silly waste of time and money! Let 'em go!"

Cleo and Mort shared a quick grin and declared they still had nothing to say. They wanted an attorney. Nigel sent them back to their cells.

"Right-O!" Nigel said after they were gone. "You were on the tack with that one, CD! This is the whole gang, outside of Israel itself. I caught the looks. They feel safe. If we let them out on bail there's no one to come after them and they have some way arranged to get out of the country.

"Now we get them to tie Shartz in to where he can't get

out. We've already set it up for Mort to be able to hear what we want heard."

"How did you do that?" LeDuc said. "We have to be sure."

"We put him in A three. If he really listens hard he can just make out what anyone in the dispatch office says – so long as it's quiet. He'll only hear snatches here and there. This can't be obvious."

We went out to get some breakfast and to discuss how we would handle it, then went back to The Yard. As we walked along the hall a man stepped out of dispatch and said Nigel was wanted by the out-agent watching number four. "He's waiting at the radio," the officer said. "I think four gave them the slip, somehow."

"I'll have some hides!" Nigel snapped. "There's hardly any way that one could ever get out of there without being seen! I'll have some hides!"

We stepped into the crowded office and closed the door. After a few minutes LeDuc opened the door and went out. Just as he opened the door Nigel said, "...to the bloody bastard! The only way he could get out without being seen is through those woods by the stream from Hamil...." The door closed, cutting him off.

About five minutes later Sir William went out, opening the door for Mort to hear the last few words he was saying. "...port. He'll have to go there. He's had time."

Mort demanded to speak with his lawyer immediately. We waited until the lawyer was there for me to go out, saying, "...you later. By now he's out of the country. I think I know how he did it, but he should be safe with the head start."

"*If* he got out then," Nigel answered. "That would mean more than ten hours head start. It had to be then! There's no other time he could get out!

"Well, he's left these with it! They'll bloody well hang! I'll see to it! Every one of the bloody bastards!

"Close the bloody damned door!"

I went on down the hall and up to the room where LeDuc and Sir William were drinking coffee and waiting. Soon Nigel came in to announce the lawyer made a fast run to see Cleo, too. As planned, the lawyer soon came to say his clients had decided to make a statement. Nigel sent a man with him to bring them to the conference room.

"It worked beautifully!" LeDuc cried. "I think I like your Yank methods!"

"Yes, I think perhaps these two innocents are going to hand us Shartz on a silver platter," Sir William said. "They think he's away and safe. They can put the whole fiasco on him. I'm interested in how they plan to get around the fact that Mort set that bomb, then detonated it – and Cleo brought both him and the bomb in."

"It'll be interesting, sure as sunset," I agreed. "Let them make their statements with the lawyer here, sign them, then we'll disclose that `four' was a stakeout watching a suspected bank robber at Hamil-Robbins. I want to see their faces!"

Chapter eleven

"I'll read your statement carefully aloud so you both can hear it, along with your attorney," Nigel said. "If it's truly your words you may sign it and we'll proceed from that point. Mr. Grimes, M. LeDuc and Sir William will be legal witnesses to the signing. This is a formal meeting and will be on record.

"Now!

"*'I, Cleo Louise Solomon, do swear and attest to the following as a true statement of the facts in the case of the placing and exploding of a device in Heathrow Airport, etc.'*

"Mortimer Bernard Solomon follows with the same oath. I'm sure your attorney has worded that oath properly and that you both understand its implications and the penalties for untruths in a sworn affidavit being felonious perjury. I see you've presented the affidavit as a general listing with following individual statements. That's good. Saves time.

"*'First, we were approached by a Mr. Auermond and a Mr. Shartz about one month ago. They represented themselves as being agents of the government of Israel, here to discuss matters of great international import with the members of the Zionist movement.*

"*'We have subsequently learned the truth of the matter is that they do not now, nor did they at that time, represent the Israeli government in any way.*

"*'Mr. Auermond and Mr. Shartz were given lodging in our home. We had no reason to mistrust them. We have always cooperated with the Israeli government in any way we could as our duty because of our Jewish heritage.*

"*'A man went there from Interpol to claim Mr. Auermond and Mr. Shartz had killed one or more persons in the United States and that they were also wanted by Interpol for various crimes of international art theft.*

"'We were vastly confused by this disclosure, but Mr. Auermond and Mr. Shartz assured us it was mistaken identity or something on that order. Mr. Auermond went to the United States immediately to try to clear up what he told us was a misunderstanding. Mr. Shartz remained at The Three Larches until Mr. Auermond's return, when they were to travel to Israel for debriefing sessions before being reassigned elsewhere.

"'We learned a short while later that Mr. Auermond had tried to kill another person in the United States and that he was in custody, as was Miss Ilya Varanov, a member of the Zionists here in London. We discovered she was also being held on a charge of attempted murder.

"'We were then vastly more confused, both because of the grave accusations against Mr. Auermond and because he would involve a friend of ours in any such venture. We did then demand that Mr. Shartz remove himself from our property and warned him we would turn him in to Interpol if he did not vacate immediately. We also expressed our outrage at the treatment his associate accorded to our dear friend, Ilya, and at his duplicity with us regarding the events stateside.

"'We were further confused and outraged by his reaction to our demands.

"'Mr. Shartz threatened to kill Mrs. Solomon if we did not allow him to stay one week more at The Three Larches. He claimed to have placed devices to destroy the house. He then claimed to be an expert on explosives and said he had placed devices to get us and our friends should his demands not find our immediate compliance. Mr. Solomon tried to force him to vacate, but he had discovered some old papers proving Mrs. Solomon had, while under the influence of certain chemicals, once joined a group called `The Workers for a Free World,

and that that group was found guilty of causing the deaths of several students at several colleges and universities during the time Mrs. Solomon was a member, though she did not then know what that group was doing.

"'She was not responsible then, and is somewhat impaired at times now due to the lasting effects of those drugs, among which was lysergic sauric diethalimide, known as LSD.

"'She felt she was still in jeopardy because of the nature of the acts that group performed. There are outstanding warrants in France and England for members of that group dating from nineteen seventy four through nineteen seventy nine. Mr. Shartz threatened to present the papers proving Mrs. Solomon's membership in that group to Scotland Yard.

"'Mr. Shartz had obtained some chemicals and materials while in London to send Mr. Auermond to the United States, which he returned to the estate. He claimed that Interpol had seized a senior member of the Israeli group he was representing in Australia or Canada and was bringing her here to London, then would take her to Paris, where she would be placed on trial and would possibly implicate Mr. Shartz in a scheme to place explosives and other terrorist devices in various places at various times.

"'Mr. Shartz made a small parcel and gave Mr. Solomon a small radio transmitter and instructions to place the package inside a trash receptacle at Heathrow and to explode it when the police and the alleged terrorist woman were close.

"'Mr. Shartz repeatedly insisted the device was small and not of much power and was meant only as a warning. Mr. Shartz said he had made many bombs of many sizes and swore to us that this one was not dangerous. It was quite small, so Mr. Solomon, not having familiarity with explosives, did not fear it.

"'Mr. Shartz made a plan whereunder Mrs. Solomon would drive the car with Mr. Solomon locked inside the boot

to Heathrow, then would go to Dublin. Mr. Solomon would place the device, detonate it, and catch the next flight to Dublin, where Mrs. Solomon would have earlier established his presence at the time of the setting off of the device.

"`Mr. and Mrs. Solomon discussed taking the device directly to New Scotland Yard and thence taking the chance the police would understand she was not a responsible person when she was a member of the old group, but the device was small and did not appear dangerous.

"`Mr. Shartz swore he would be gone when they returned to The Three Larches if the device was set off as agreed. He further intimated he would destroy the papers so foolishly retained by Mrs. Solomon implicating her with The Workers for a Free World.

"`At no time did either Cleo or Mortimer Solomon know or even suspect that the device was dangerous. Their actions were the result of blackmail by Mr. Shartz. They were under constant and unceasing duress and extreme mental strain.

"`When the device exploded and killed three people Mr. Solomon panicked and went to Dublin and his wife where both were arrested and returned to London.'

"The individual statements say neither knew the danger of the bomb and that they were not operating under their own free will. Is that a true reading?"

Both Cleo and Mort agreed that it was, so they signed it and we witnessed. Nigel called in an officer to take the statements and file them. "And have seven bring Shartz in," he said as the officer left the room. "We have the testimony that he made the bloody damned bombs they used – here and other places. That will hang him sure! I'll watch him swing with glee!"

"Seven?!" Mort exploded. "Wha..!? I mean, I would think Shartz would be long gone!"

"Oh, we've been keeping a very close eye on that one,"

Nigel replied innocently. "There's no way he could go any-where."

"But I heard you ... I mean, there was a lot of yelling – I thought he had escaped!" Mort cried "There was a lot of yelling earlier about him getting away!"

"We wanted to get our statements to you quickly so he wouldn't escape the country," Cleo said quickly. "Shut up, Mortie dear. We want to be sure Shartz gets exactly what he deserves for what he did to us!"

"There was no yelling about anyone getting away!" Sir William said indignantly. "We would never yell about any such thing if it ever *did* happen! What are you ranting about?"

"Mort overheard about someone escaping in the woods toward Hamilton," Cleo said. "It changes nothing. We were going to give the statements, just not this soon. We were afraid he would blow up the house and we wanted to be sure the old papers were gone forever, though I would suppose there were other records of them. That's why I kept mine.

"You see, they elected me their president – and I didn't even know about it! I never knew anything about the club! I thought we were going to protest the Yanks in Vietnam and the atomic tests and that sort of thing!"

"There was never mention of anyone around Hamilton at all," Nigel said. "I don't think...."

"Ha! You were the best president they ever had!" Mort snapped at her. "They said four's hide would be stripped for letting him get away! It was just a trick, wasn't it?"

"Four?" Nigel said. "Great god! Four was watching that Bob Warner fellow who's supposed to be part of the Bank of England robbery where they killed those two drivers! That's at Hamil-Robbins, not Hamilton! How did you hear that? I want to know – and right *now*! I want no information leaks here! I won't tolerate loose lips in this department!"

"I could hear from the dispatch office in my cell," Mort

said. "I want police protection until Shartz is brought in, then I want safe conduct somewhere! They'll get me for this! Now she has to shut *me* up! I'll turn state's evidence for a protection deal!" he was sweating profusely and was a sickly white.

"But I don't know what he's talking about!" Cleo cried. "What state's evidence? What have you been hiding from me?!"

"Oh, *no*!" he shot back acidly. "I've been going on all these years pretending you're my wife, but I'm not playing this game one more step! This thing started turning sour a long time ago! Officers, I only married her for the cause. We've stayed in the same bedroom only at those times we've had company not of the group. Cleo Solomon is head of enforcement and publicity – which is to say intimidation and terrorism – for the group, The Workers for a Free World, which is still going strong. She's in charge of all European operations.

"I was once idealistic as hell, but I'm bloody well a cynic now! I'll turn state's evidence all bloody right! You bet! I'll turn state's evidence against *her*!"

"I think the poor dear has suffered a nervous breakdown from all this stress," Cleo said confidentially. "He's been acting very strangely ever since Mr. Auermond and Mr. Shartz came to stay in our house. These accusations are silly!"

"I don't think they're silly at all," I snarled. "I think we can show there's no way you could be blackmailed about any group in the seventies and you damned well know it. I think Varanov, Overberg, Auermond and Shartz will all want to make deals. I believe your decision to kill off the best operative you had, Carla Sohn, was the mistake that'll do you in. That was going 'way too far! They all know very well you'll sacrifice them in a heartbeat! I think a man in Gainesville, Florida, will tell me he was gunning for you all along. He as much as told me that the first time we met.

"In case you haven't figured it by now, Shartz will very obviously make both your statements perjury."

"Jenkins! Come in here!" Nigel ordered through the intercom.

When the officer came he said to take Cleo to her cell and to see she was watched twenty four hours a day, then to call the prosecutor's office to have a top man sent over to discuss a deal with Mort. LeDuc said he'd arrange to have prosecutors from other countries there, too. A deal with Mort would put a permanent end to this branch of the group, if it *wouldn't* stop it altogether.

I stayed only long enough to see that all the ends were tied. Shartz read Cleo's affidavit putting the whole thing right on him (while not mentioning she thought he had made his escape when she gave the testimony) and couldn't say nearly enough against her. He even gave the names of people he made bombs for in Australia, Canada and Hong Kong. Overberg also caved in, but they had the secret room and all those weapons to use as leverage on him.

I loaded the jet, said my goodbyes and headed home, where I spent a week with my family and for some fishing before going to call on Yusef Kharavor.

"I will tell you a story," Yusef said, buttering the hot pecan Danish lavishly. "You may make of it what you will.

"Remember when I told you one needs the wiles of a Cleopatra and the wisdom of a Solomon to keep some things going for any period of time?"

"Yes," I answered, buttering my own Danish. We were sitting in the restaurant not far from his warehouse where I first saw him. "That struck me all of a sudden a few days ago. It was the reason I told Nigel and Sir William it would be a bad idea to offer Cleo immunity in a deal."

He smiled expansively, took a sip of the strong coffee and

said, "So! To a fairytale!

"Once upon a time a boy was born in a place of dry, rocky land. His parents were able to subsist by raising a few goats and some poor vegetables and with the father working part of the time in a small village nearby, doing whatever was called for at the time. There had recently been a great war, a world war it was called, and times were difficult for all.

"The boy was raised and given an education by his parents and by the small school in the village that taught only reading and writing and numbers.

"As time went on, conditions in the small town slowly improved and the people prospered. There was water found in deep wells that would allow crops to be grown for better and more varied food supplies. The parents of the boy were able to give him more than they themselves ever had. Yes, they gave him a few *things* but, most importantly, they gave him great love.

"Since the great war, a small nation was established nearby for a people who had been without a nation of their own for many centuries. These people were greatly resented in the whole area, for they had never earned a nation. They had spent much of their history living among many other nations and had gained a great reputation for ability in business and brilliance in several sciences, then had solidly established themselves in the businesses in which they specialize. They have always been seen as great natural manipulators of money. They have a truly uncanny ability to accumulate and use money.

"As those people have a racial psychology of expansion and accumulation, then exclusion of others, they brought that with them into this new nation and soon that nation had no friends anywhere – except for the country who helped to establish them.

"The boy in our story was much confused. The country

who had established this nation claimed that the area was the historical homeland of the people who moved there and claimed that gave them the right to the place, yet the country who established them had seized their own land from the natives to establish their own nation – land which had historically never even seen their people in all of time! That nation treated the natives badly. They saw no reason why their country was the natives' historical homeland gave them any rights whatever!

"How could that be?

"Much of the territory this nation who established the new nation occupied was wrested from the natives in bloody warfare a short time past, while the established nation in this rocky, dry place had not known the land in many centuries, yet these people had historical rights while those who had been put in preserves after their land was taken only a few years ago had no historical rights?

"How could that be?

"The people native to the area where this new nation was established knew of the acquisitive nature of the people moved there from many places and always knew there would be great and continuing trouble. One nation, defeated in the world war, had badly mistreated those people coming to the new nation. That was given as reason to establish the new nation and the people moving there vowed never to permit such an evil nation to again arise on the face of the Earth – yet they were more and more acting like that evil nation they had so recently vowed never to forget!

"All the boy's life he was taught the evil nation had done many terrible and atrocious things out of frustration with the psychology and ways of the people of this new nation. They had, as was their nature, first acquired great supplies of money and had entered into business, then had shut out the other people in the country from those businesses.

"Much of this affected the boy's little village, now quite prosperous, very little. The people living in the village conducted the business of life on their own. They bothered no one and were bothered by no one. The father built a small business of his own, trading in furniture and other household goods. He became wealthy enough to send his children to that wonderful country across a wide sea so they could become free and would have the great opportunity to build a good life for themselves. It was the same nation who had established the new nation nearby, which was now becoming ever more belligerent to its neighbors, using the same tactics the evil nation who so oppressed them used not so very many years before, claiming they were being threatened as excuse to attack their neighbors.

"The father of the boy wanted his children to explain these things to the country where they now lived who had established the belligerent new nation. The country would not hear of it. It refused to hear anything evil about the new nation. There were many people of the same race as the new country there who were very wealthy and powerful businessmen who could command great amounts of publicity. The people from the nearby areas had no wealth or power, so were not heard.

"A great philosopher once said that none are so blind as those who will not see nor so deaf as those who will not hear. That saying applies to countries as well as to individuals.

"The rocky land of the area where the boy was born and raised was taken by the new belligerent nation when the weak surrounding nations tried to attack the new nation. The attack was in true reality the same kind of attack that the new nation regularly made – and still makes – against its neighbors. It was an attack in selfdefense. It was an attack against an acquisitive neighbor who cares only about things and not about the people.

"The nation who established the new country would not see or hear anything evil about its own creation, even when that new country was as arrogant and obstructive to them! They gave them ever more and stood with them against the entire rest of the world!

"Soon, as is the nature of these people, there were spies sent from the new nation into the country who originally established and supported them by the taxing of its own people. There were even squads sent from various factions in the new country to many other countries around the world to do their mischief. Still, the country who had established and nurtured them would not see and would not hear.

"There are many good people in this new country who now become steadily more alarmed and frightened by what their country has become, but they cannot be heard. They have no power. They are shut out by their leaders much as the others were always shut out in business in other countries for all of their history. They've become as much slaves to this evil thing, as are the people in the area who were taken.

"The Nazis were a minority who controlled their people without choices of those to be governed. There were no elections such as are held in this new nation to elect the leaders who do these things.

"The evil nation in the great war was reviled for racism. Now this new nation is racist in a far worse way – they are racist against even their own kind. The old evil nation was greatly reviled for censoring and controlling the press and other public media of their own nation as well as of others – now this new nation does the same thing. The evil nation was reviled for oppressing all who came under their influence – now this new nation does the same. The evil nation was reviled for murdering the people of this new nation – their women and children, not warriors. Now this new nation does the same. The evil nation was reviled for attacking its neighbors with contrived excuses – now this new nation does the same thing. The evil nation was reviled for destroying homes, churches and businesses of the people who did not share its philosophy – now this new nation does the same thing.

"The list goes on and on.

"The boy with whom this story is concerned found himself to be impotent to do anything. No one would see him. No one would hear him.

"The boy met many new friends in his new homeland. He had some other family there, too, and many of his new friends were the same race as the new nation and were horrified at what it was becoming, yet they, also, had no voice anywhere in the new nation *or* in this great nation who had established the new country. The people were embarrassed and ashamed at what the new nation was becoming and were outraged because there were now spies and worse being sent even against this country who was supporting the new nation.

"The boy, now a grown man with a family of his own, was in a business that dealt with many people in many other lands. He was able to obtain much information about many things, among them was who some of the worst of the spies and terrorists coming from the new nation were. There was little he could do. His first priority was to aid his own people back in the old land, but there was so little....

"Then one day a friend of the boy, who we will call Ralph – because that name is as good as any – came to say he had an idea that could result in food for people everywhere in places like the old homeland. The food could be grown using salt water, which was plentiful. It was all based on a new science. The food would be used to feed all people and would remove the weapon of food forever from evil hands!

"The boy had a young nephew who was an expert in electronic devices and who was conversant with other forms of science. This nephew would be there to report to the boy all that happened. The boy joyfully gave all he could to Ralph to start this wonderful thing.

"Another good lady, who we will call Sylvia – because that name is as good as any – matched the boy's funds and the place was started!

"Ralph was a very good man. He was also, as are many good men, too trusting. He hired a scientist who we will call Nora and her husband, who we will call George – which are names as good as any – who were good choices, as the woman was brilliant and the man was smart and useful.

"Another, who we will call Gus, came with them because of a good recommendation. Ralph, being a very trusting person, gave Gus a job.

"The boy knew Gus was not to be trusted because he was one of the blind and deaf of the country and he was of the race of the new nation. He was possibly a good man, but he was a foolish man, who, like Ralph, trusted too much. He also foolishly thought the ends justify the means, a thing all history has disproven many times in many ways.

"There was no danger. Everything was going well. The research was proving profitable and some progress was being made, but the research drew attention of some of the spies of the new nation. It was showing potential to produce food both easily and cheaply. The spies and their faction viewed this as a weapon to be used to oppress people everywhere, so they used deceit to get Gus to give them an important discovery. The nephew saw this, but too late. I said Ralph was too trusting. This was proof.

"You see, there was an agent of the new nation, who we will call Carson – because that name is as good as any – who had early insinuated himself into the project. The boy still knows not how he learned of the research, but Carson saw the potential of the project and the possibility of using it as a weapon. It was this Carson person who brought in the spies and their trickery. The boy saw what was happening then. His contacts in other places warned him that Carson was not as he seemed, but it was too late. Carson was already part of the project.

"The boy decided to play their own game against them. He made a plan then to destroy this group of which Carson and the spies were so important a part. He used some of his own contacts in another nation to make the leader of the spy group suspicious of Carson. There were hints and evidences planted with this leader, who we will call Cleo – because that name is as good as any – to make her think this Carson person was going to try to take her leadership away from her, so she sent a trusted comrade to watch Carson on the false premise that the watcher was wanted for many crimes elsewhere and needed a place to stay where no one would look for her.

"The boy made plans to get the research Gus had given to the spies back for his people, but he needed to cause a distraction. The fruits of that research were now in the new nation. Plans were made for any time a distraction arose and, I'm proud to say, the boy's plan has very recently proven successful when the death of the woman who was watching Carson took the attention of two people and made them leave the research they were watching for a few minutes. The research is being planted now in other places. Thus is that weapon thwarted.

"This is about the boy, not the research.

"Things went back to normal. The nephew discovered the ruse the spies used to get into the research areas and was watching them very carefully. Nora was successful in the basic steps to make plants grow in salt water.

"Then the nephew discovered Gus was stealing the research and was meeting with the spies! This was the big thing, not just some tomato seeds!

"The nephew quickly contacted the boy, who insisted the theft of the research by those people must be stopped in any way possible, while the research must be completed. He charged the nephew with going as far as killing Gus, should that prove to be the only way.

"Too soon that was the only way. Now these people had made a murderer out of the nephew, therefore, the boy shared the guilt of that equally, but there was no shame! The research was safe and was returned to Nora, who would finish it! The boy had been successful!

"Then the spies killed naive, trusting, good, Ralph and a pain, rage and guilt that will never end descended upon the boy. That was too much for the boy to tolerate, so he made another plan.

"He learned through the nephew that a very famous and fair famous private detective, we will call him CD – because that name is as good as any – was already on the case. The boy knew his friend, Ralph, would be avenged, but he also knew there was a way to cause the whole group of which the spies were a part to be destroyed, at the same time. The boy got word to the leader that Carson would be found out and would tell all, that there was a lever the police could use that she knew nothing about. The watcher was there and was an experienced killer, so Cleo had Carson removed as any possible problem either then or in the future. It was perfect! The boy knew great glee!

"The spies escaped to another country when CD was carefully misdirected. It was important they go to the leader so CD could be steered there later.

"The nephew handed the police and CD the evidence proving the spies had murdered Ralph and admitted to the killing of Gus. CD, being the man he is, went to bring the spies to justice. He was able to figure where the watcher was going and to have her abducted and held until he could cause the spies to come back to face the justice of the land where they killed Ralph.

"The boy planted some ideas in the leader's mind, making her very suspicious of one of the spies, so she used a ruse to send yet another of the group with one spy to America while the other would remain in the country of her residence to make devices for the watcher to use when she returned.

"The spy who went to America was caught, as was the one who went with him. The watcher was caught by Interpol and was even then being returned to the country where the leader resided. The boy planted the idea in the leader that the watcher was preparing to tell all to save herself. Cleo was soon convinced a deal had been made.

"You see, the boy was using the husband of Cleo to reach her. He had met the husband many years ago and had become interested in him because he was married to Cleo, who was at that time a member of a terrorist organization that had been posing as a Free World Society. The boy pretended to be sympathetic to the society and was a secret source of information to the husband, so had great influence.

"The second thing went terribly wrong. First time was when Ralph was killed, now two innocent men were killed when Cleo got rid of the watcher. The boy has wept much over that.

"CD, as the boy knew, was exceptionally ingenious. He was able to capture Cleo, her husband and, as a bonus, the one who had supplied the terrorists with their materials. The boy is now satisfied. Justice is done.

"He will know pain, grief and guilt for the rest of his life because Ralph and those two innocent men died as a result of his scheming. A much greater good was done, so it is something that must be. Perhaps there are those times when the end justifies the means. History will judge.

"That is the story told. I hope you found it entertaining."

I thought a minute, then said, "Perhaps the boy should wonder if perhaps *he* is now using the methods he so deplores? Perhaps the boy will realize that this sort of thing must feed on itself and that he has let the end justify the means in a way history will judge harshly?

"There is guilt enough to go around. Arafat views the story from his place and Cleo views it from hers. I hope *we* both view it from closer to the truth that's somewhere between the extremes presented. I can't say, had I lived inside the problem as you and your family have, that I would have done any different. The world will know in a hundred years or so – if it lasts that much longer.

"I think I'm satisfied with it too, really. It's done.

"I've got to get the recipe for these pecan Danishes!"

"I think if CD asks the nephew about what Gus said before he died he may see many things more clearly," Yusef said. "They are good, aren't they?"

Chapter twelve

"I think that story tells me a great deal about what I need to know," I said. "I was wondering if this was a plan of yours all along."

"Only since Ralph's death, so far as you're concerned. I saw the great new opportunity, so seized it. I could not allow it to pass. I no longer have any extensive knowledge of what is happening at the gene labs or with Eduard. I deeply hope and trust you will understand why he has done what he has done and I hope you will see fit to allow the charges to stand against the spy, Auermond."

"We have very little choice about that. If we change anything now he can appeal and will get away with killing Ralph. I've decided Eisingstein, regardless of anything else, was acting in such a way that he was technically a traitor to this country. His intentions were probably good, but he was acting for a foreign power, even if he wasn't being tricked by Auermond and Shartz. If he wanted to hold any allegiances to Israel he should have renounced his citizenship here."

"It is very sad. Gus was an intelligent person, in many ways, but he was terribly misguided. Many are. The truth is generally not known here, but I have to admit it is because the people here do not care to see the truth. I see in this morning's papers that an eleven year old child was killed and seventeen people, mostly pre-teens, were injured. The story was in a small item in a list on page six of section three.

"After all the things that are known and after daily having these items placed on the back pages of secondary sections the USA is still to Israel what Mussolini was to Hitler. It is very sad. There are so many Jews who are clearly outraged by the behavior of Israel's army and its leaders. History does not treat such leaders well.

"Look up Hitler.

"Look up Mussolini.

"My friend, we were able to stop a very small part of this thing.

"There is a small part of the story I have left out. We can call this part `Fairytale Part Two: The Sequel.' It takes place in the period between the start of part one and the time Ralph starts his project.

"Our hero, the boy in part one, is now in the country across the sea. It is the time shortly after the new nation has taken the town of the parents of the boy. The father of the boy still has a small business and is doing well, but some evil people from the occupying country want his business. As is their nature, they want to accumulate money and things and to shut the natives out from the business.

"But what can they do? Opinion in much of the world is already against them. They can't seize the business as they have done so often before. The outcry is growing.

"There is a solution! There is a way!

"There is an organization known as `Workers for a Free World' – and there is an extreme radical Zionist who is president of that organization. They are much experienced in terrorism, called `Freedom fighting' if the ones who do it are leaders of the new nation, a tactic used by the evil nation in part one.

"This organization is called in by the businessmen of the new nation and the situation is explained. There is a bombing which happens to destroy the businesses along a narrow lane through the peaceful village, among those businesses the one belonging to the father of the boy across the sea. The bombing, as they are often designed to do, is called a terrorist act, which it was, but is blamed on the people who lost all in the bombing.

"The father of the boy across the sea makes a protest

against the bombing, thus is now becoming a problem to these businessmen, so he is accused of hiding the very same people who destroyed his business – and his house is bulldozed to the ground. It is yet another act of terrorism, but it is to be excused, even though that excuse is a study in true illogic. People become afraid to protest and the father is left with nothing – yet he continues to protest. In a final act of intimidation and terrorism the father is jailed for not paying taxes on the destroyed home and business. He remains to this day in jail, while the woman who was president of the hired terrorist organization goes back to England with her expert who places the bombs and helps her in making the false accusations. The ones who made the terror bombs go to the same country across the sea where the boy is living. Nothing is resolved. Nothing is settled. Nothing changes.

"The sequel should, perhaps, come before the fairytale, yes?"

"Yes. The next sequel would possibly be when the wicked witch who was the president of the terrorist organization is caught, the placer of bombs is executed by the wicked witch and her friends, the maker of the bombs is executed in another far country and the others in the terrorist group are placed in a dark dungeon for all time. That will be the last of this particular tale until there is justice for the father of the boy across the sea, but, to tell the truth, I don't think that will ever be. No one will live happily ever after in this tale."

"My friend, I fear greatly that you are right. For things to change would entail a change in nature of several diverse peoples and a desire for truth among the people in the land across the sea where the boy resides. Perhaps the truth is not as the boy sees it, but it is also not as those people see it. Anywhere between is still intolerable by any standards of humanity, but only when you speak of humanity as an ideal, not as it is.

"We make small changes. We do what we can."
"Yeah. We do what we can."

"So it all comes back to the fact that Yusef Kharavor's parents were set up by these same people?" Len asked as we all sat on the terrace at my Englewood home eating a snack Alma threw together – fried clams, fried oysters, fried fish sticks, pork and beans (*always* with fried seafood!), shrimp, hushpuppies and mustard greens.

"As close as doesn't make any difference," I answered. "He saw me come in, knew all about me and manipulated the events to make me do what I had to do. The first time I went up to Gainesville to meet him I scared hell out of him."

"That's true!" Ed Vore said. "You didn't do one thing he tried to get you to do there. He thought he'd miscalculated completely and would end up getting me electrocuted! It was a strange situation. It still is.

"I would gladly announce to the world I was the one who killed Gus. I'm not ashamed of that, even though I liked him, in a lot of ways. It was a thing that had to be done. If I do that the killer of Ralph Meiner, who was a very good man, will eventually go free. I must remain silent for the very reasons you mustn't reveal I was his assassin.

"Life is strange."

"You can say that again!" JK said. "We learned a hell of a lot about security systems and those kinds of computers! I think we could tie a system over the fax network...." He got dreamy-eyed, stood and wandered into my study to plug my PC into the fax line on the safe phone. Tony grinned and shrugged.

"That kid is strange!" Alma declared. "We were talking about hybridizing orchids the other day. I'd explained the method the records were kept and how we put everything on the computer. He watched me fill out a tag for a cross I'd made, got that weird look and wandered away. I saw him in the study a couple of hours later, but didn't pay any attention. He brought me a list of the primary characteristics I could expect from the cross. He worked out a way to let the computer tell us what we'd get so we wouldn't have to bother with half the stuff we cross."

"I don't think it'll work too well," Ed said.

"I agree. CD and I discussed it a couple of years ago," Tony said. "It'll give such a low probability factor it would make it unreasonable to make a lot of crosses for the commercial market, but it can't predict the one super spectacular plant out of a cross that's otherwise pointless."

"Like that green and bronze thing Alma crossed, the one she calls Blc. Stupidity. It predicted just what we got for ninety nine percent of them, but it didn't predict the two plants out of the three hundred we grew that are the most spectacular bronze/greens I ever saw!" I said. "That Blc. Stupidity `Bronze Perfection' FCC and the variety `Superba' weren't anywhere in the equations. They made the cross worth making fifty times over."

"It's as hard to predict people," Jim Barrow said. "You can't go by what's true of ninety nine percent of them. It won't hold true on the hundredth – against any possible way to figure it."

"Well, Yusef predicted this one very well," Len pointed out. "Auermond got two life sentences, the first without parole, *then* he starts the second. As soon as he's dead he'll be eligible for parole – after twenty five years!

"Nigel asked me to tell you Shartz got forty four years in England, then went to France where he got forty more, then went to Spain where they're going to put him against a wall and shoot him, rendering the other sentences a wee tad irrelevant. I guess he can start the English sentence as soon as they ship the body back."

"Sir William called me last night," I said. "Overberg, the one who was supplying the basic materials to the bombers and other friendly neighborhood – stress the hood – terrorists, got forty years for the bomb materials and a total of three hundred twenty one more for the automatic weapons and missile launchers or whatever."

"Well, I just hope we got all of them this time," Cal said. "Pass the hushpuppies, please.

"I can't figure how you were so easy to manipulate, CD. Yusef seems to have played you like a Stradivarius!"

"Oh, Cal!" Wilma cried. "He was doing it to everyone. He's very good at it – and CD *did* figure it out.

"Why *did* you continue after you found out, CD?"

"Simple. By then, I'd solved the murder of Gus, which was my only real responsibility. I saw we wouldn't be able to tag Ed for that because things were already looking out of kilter. I was mad as hell because Meiner was killed in what seemed a random act and knew very well, deep inside, that Ed had nothing to do with that. Yusef was trying to steer me to Auermond, also obviously, but he had already seen to it that Auermond was out of the country.

"Let's face it! I was curious! Ed showed me beyond doubt that Auermond killed Ralph and had admitted to killing Gus. I could already see why we couldn't untie the two that way or any decent lawyer would have the whole mess thrown out of any court in the world. Yusef said something about the wiles of a Cleopatra and the wisdom of Solomon. I saw the name Solomon several times in the lists we'd been going over, so I couldn't let that go! – Besides, I wanted to go to England, anyhow. I just said, `OK, pal! Let's see what the hell you're up to.'

"Quite honestly, I'm glad I did. We got them all, I think."

"Not quite yet," Dave suggested.

I'd forgotten he was there sitting on the floor to one side of the table.

"How do you figure?" Len asked.

"There's one little information lapse. It may mean nothing whatever or maybe I didn't catch the explanation when it came around. It has to do with the timing. Maybe Nora Seely can clear it up.

"You see, there was never any connection between Gus Eisingstein and any of this mess until she suddenly recommended him for the job. She said he had done some things, but so had thousands of others. If it was a matter of reading about him in the trade journals, then his being asked to join the crew was a one in a million chance. The fact he was tied up in this whole bunch, Carson Wilder to Auermond and Shartz, is totally ridiculous if you want me to believe it was coincidental.

"Who's in the woodwork here? Who put Nora onto Gus?"

"Fair question," I said, and went to the phone. I knew Nora was at the lab inputting her process into the fax machines to be sent all over the world. No one wanted any profit from this one. The lab was going to continue with Ed running the administration end with George's help. They already had hundreds of applications to fill other positions, now that the process was completed and known. The only thing needed now was research into making the plants grow better – and to test for toxins and such that often enter the genetic equation.

George answered and said he didn't know, so he called Nora and put her on. She said she had the application in her files and would call back in a few minutes.

"CD? He was recommended by the `Green Revolution Committee' in England," she said when she called back. "I read about his work in the journals, knew he was local, so I called him in. He seemed a bit surprised, but was very happy with the final arrangement. Why? Is it important?"

"Do you get recommendations through that sort of place

often?"

"Yes. Always! They're groups who try to get people who are concerned with ecology and causes into the positions where they can make a difference. They save us a lot of time, expense, paperwork and interviews by sending a complete resume' along with the application."

"But you say Gus was surprised?"

"Not unusual. The groups keep tabs on people with certain basic ideas and recommend them. Usually they have several names on the lists, but this one only has the one. I assumed he was the only one local. I liked the resume' and called him. We talked. I told Ralph and it was done."

"Thanks. We were just curious."

Dave was watching me and saw the look in my eyes.

"I think maybe I have to go back to England. I want to know everything there is to know about some bunch called the `Green Revolution Committee' there. I want to know if it has another name – like maybe `The Workers for a Free World!'"

"JK! Comeeraminit!" Tony called.

JK came out with a roll of printout paper in his hand.

"Find out everything there is to know about a worldwide ecological organization known as `Green Revolution Committee' operating out of England," Tony said.

JK nodded and went back inside. Tony grinned and shrugged and Ed went in to help. Cal took another serving of clams and gave more to Wilma. Len took more pork and beans and mustard greens. I got another large serving of fried oysters. Dave was figuring something on a piece of paper and Alma poured some more iced tea.

We waited.

"Uh, GRC is one of those protest groups who want to stop all atomic bomb tests, nuclear power, cutting rain forests and a lot of good stuff," JK reported. "They get nutzo to the point we'd all eat organic foods and ride horses, even if the calculations show the excrement of the horses would be thirty feet deep all over the world with present population levels – except I could figure how many people would die of starvation because the bugs would eat all the crops.

"OK, Tony. Don't look at me like that.

"The movement started a few years ago in Canada, then moved its main headquarters to Australia when a Mrs. Armundstedt was elected their president. Some guy named Mortimer Solomon is the present ... hey! Isn't that the Cleo broad's husband?"

"How do they operate here?" Dave asked with a smug expression on his face.

"They mostly recommend things. Like, they sent letters to the whale committee for Dr. Reed, so he was put in charge. He's pretty good. They recommended Dr. Jonas for the moisture retention project in New Mexico. He seems to be doing very well. They're pushing Lars Nordstrum on the Brazillian rain forest conservation board. They seem really intent on getting Dr. Bilstein on the desert reforestation project. All of them seem the best qualified for the jobs."

"Looks normal on the surface, but I wonder why Mort's in it ... Armundstedt? Armundstedt? ... She was the first president to move the operation? Connie Armundstedt?" I asked.

"Yeah. The bomber broad," Ed said from the doorway. "I checked on the basic credentials of all the people they recommend and guess what?"

"The one on the moisture retention project – that's to develop something that will hold moisture in desert soils that plants can take the water from, but that stops most evaporation – and the one on desert reforestation fit the basic psychological profile of Gus Eisingstein," Dave smirked.

"Rabidly pro-Israel?" Cal asked. "I see! Get a man in those places who'll sell out to a story that he's doing it for Israel! Just what happened with Gus!"

"And use it to keep power in those countries," Tony agreed. "All these things being developed for the good of the whole human race are to be stolen and later used as weapons against poor countries Israel considers as being their enemies and Israel considers everyone on this planet except the US – and only part of us – enemies."

"Yup! Control the food and you control the world," Jim said. "That's what the scorched Earth policy was all about. It's an old idea.

"You know what that means?"

"Oh, Yeah!" I answered. "It means once the data and research are stolen the one who actually did it has to go. Nora would've been killed if Auermond and Shartz had gotten that research from Gus."

"Gus *had* to know that fact," Dave pointed out. "You waste your tears on that miserable excuse for a miserable excuse. He would put the life of a brilliant scientist like her in jeopardy for a chance to advance Israel?

"Before you try to argue he thought the whole world would get the research if he gave it to Israel, stop to think. If that were true he wouldn't have gone to the extremes he did to steal it. Nora, Ed, Ralph and George had already stated they would only charge enough to pay the investors – and Sylvia and Yusef said they weren't interested in any money from that project. Israel could have gotten it for five percent of those funds they have publicly *offerred* to pay for that kind of thing! Eisingstein knew perfectly well the process was to be used to subjugate even more people in the East. He thought it was Israel who would do it and not that radical bunch."

"No! Gus thought Israel would do no wrong!" Alma cried. "He wouldn't be part of that!"

"Ah-ah! Gus thought Israel *could* do no wrong," Cal corrected. "If they were doing something like that it had to be right. He saw nothing wrong with killing children or bull-dozing houses or with censoring the press – so long as it was *Israel* who was doing it!

"Think for a minute. He knew perfectly damned well those tomatoes he gave them weren't being given to anyone."

"You want to tell us what he said to you before you stuck him, Ed?" Dave asked. "I'll bet you figured no one would ever believe you, so you didn't volunteer anything."

Ed looked around at us, shrugged and said, "He said Israel had to be determined and had to resist its natural feelings of revulsion when it stopped the research or its enemies would swarm down and engulf it. He said it was Israel alone against the whole world and Israel could beat them all if it held to its resolve. He said a new age was coming on Earth and that there wasn't room for both Arabs and Israelis on that great new world. He said god would stand beside Israel until every last pagan and heretic was in the hell they so deserved. The land of plenty was at hand and Israel must seize the initiative or be destroyed.

"Gus was nothing at all like the person we'd all thought he was. I discovered that when I listened to the conversations he had with Auermond and Shartz. I didn't give anyone those tapes. I erased all but one of them because with him dead and the research back in Nora's hands it would serve no useful purpose."

"That tape shows Auermond and Shartz taking orders from Gus, not from Cleo?" I asked.

"Yes. Cleo gave the orders to Gus, but Gus gave the orders to Auermond and Shartz. I thought that would be kind of obvious from the tapes showing them leaving the vault after I killed Gus."

"You had a point of view from what you already knew the

others didn't have," Dave said.

"It always seemed a bit incongruous to me," Len said. "They came out of that vault worried about it being a trap to get *them*! They weren't worried that *they* would be the logical ones to be used as a trap for *Gus*! Damn! All along we had that, but we didn't see it!"

"We didn't want to see it," I said. "We're as bad about this as most people are about what's happening over there. We gloss over a hidden little item in section `C' about Arab teenagers being shot by Israeli troops in the occupied areas and reporters being ordered out and we gloss over something like that scene at the vault. We don't want Israel to be what it is and we didn't want Gus to be a slimeball who'd sell the lives of his co-workers for a stupid ideal. We simply won't learn, will we?"

"We don't want to learn," Jim agreed. "So what's new? When was it ever any different? At which point did we ever actually learn one single solitary damned thing from history?

"Pass the hushpuppies. I'll eat those last two if no one else wants them."

"You'll just say `so what?' and change the subject?" Ed asked.

"Why get all het up about it?" Jim asked. "We've all done what we can in the situation. All this was about is being sure you didn't miss any of them. You didn't. What're you gonna change by beating your breast and crying `Mea culpa' now? There aren't any more in this bunch and you aren't gonna start any movement that'll change anything here. I'd be willing to bet your Uncle Yusef might do a little something.

"You have to realize, no one here is involved like you are. Our families are here and safe, for the moment, so it's one of those displaced things. It's one of the tactics the Nazis used then and the Israelis use now. You can get people all upset over any one of the many killings of those kids over there, but if they kill enough of them it becomes `My! How terribly sad and unfortunate!' Our minds reject anything over three as having any real importance unless we're directly involved."

"You're a lot deeper than you seem, sometimes," Dave said to Jim, grinning. "We each have our nature. Stereotypes may be embarrassing or demeaning, but they're stereotypes because a lot of the race or creed or whatever being placed in them *do* act that way. That's something we can't change, either. Individually, we can say we won't do or say something that tends to place us inside the stereotype, but the group will do the same and act the same so we'll be *identified* as being that way, too, if we're part of the group in question. That's a fact of life we have to live with and I don't have any sympathy for people who run around crying about being stereotyped. If they act differently they'll actually be raised in the observer's view for being strong enough of character to overcome it. Never forget *you're* part of a stereotyped group, too. That's where your own point of view generally comes from! Consider it and you won't make an ass of yourself quite so often. Sometimes. Maybe.

"I asked about that because there was a possibility of another group or force behind it, but it was the same group. They had established their movement for the one express purpose of being able to get a specific type into a specific place at a specific time so they could direct the situation. Most people are innately lazy. They rely on those groups when they need new personnel because the groups will screen the applicants for them – and it doesn't hurt a damned thing to have a little extra public support for a project. The groups can rally that for you. You kill two birds and all those cliche's.

"I don't think you've considered the likelihood that the salt resistance thing might make the foods inedible. The break-through was made, so it'll come.

"Just to be a bastard about it, what if the murders were all for nothing from *any* point of view? Inserting those genes changes the nature of the compounds the plant produces.

"We'll see. We can hope it works out well. If you've read any of my crap you know my feelings about overpopulation. I'm not sure it's a good idea to find things to encourage ever more population on an already overstressed ecology. In fact, I think it's stupid!

"I have to respect Yusef Kharavor, though I've never met the man. He's imparted to Ed here his own philosophy. Ed and Yusef are Arabs, but they don't condemn all Jews for no more reason than their being Jews. Yusef was incensed because Ralph, who he considered a good friend as well as a great man, was killed. CD said he actually wept because Ralph was killed and felt deep guilt and shame because it was the result of his own plan going awry.

"Yusef judges people, but he judges them individually and only according to what they show him and not from hearsay or standard stereotypes. I imagine he would be as hard on other Arabs as he is on Zionists if he were over there. He would as quickly demand that Ed kill another Palestinian who was doing harm to his people as he would to kill a thing such as Gus. (Ed nodded and said, "Harder. A lot harder.")

"There's a great danger in that. He isn't infallible. He could judge someone wrongly. His personal feelings of guilt wouldn't change what would happen."

"I read something like that in the SF Quarterly Review!" JK said. "This robot, Tab, said something like that. It isn't enough that a person judges another honestly and fairly, he has no right to judge him wrongly! Did you read that, too?"

"He wrote it. He writes those Maita books."

"Gee! You sure could use some education about modern computers for that stuff! Tab could do a lot more than you have him doing."

He blushed and grinned sheepishly. Dave grinned. Tony

grinned and shrugged. Cal sniggered (Cal does *not* like Dave, though they try to get along).

Wilma gave Cal a dirty look, Dave looked amused, Alma picked up the dishes, Ed looked uncomfortable and I thought it was going to be another very interesting night!

"Well, it seems to have checked out," Tony greeted as I went into the offices of Crane in the morning. "We checked all the suggestions the committee recommended and found every single one of them in a sensitive area were the same type. Gus was a big gun in the committee.

"Mortimer Solomon is telling them anything they want to know about any subject. He reports Gus started that scam a few years ago as a way to get their hands on major projects before anyone else got a chance at them. They've probably gotten a thing or two in the past, but this was the big one."

"I talked with Sir William last night," I said "He reports that they've really cleaned the whole gang up in England and in France. There could still be one or two of them in Australia and Canada, but strictly second-raters who'll crawl back under their individual rocks.

"M. LeDuc found a set of folders in code at The Three Larches. Mort knew part of the code and they were able to break it. It'll tell about every one of their little pet projects, but the really important part is that it tells about the part of the gang in Israel. The Israeli government is going to act against a few of them who were too extreme even for them to excuse.

"I had Sir William, Nigel and LeDuc make a conference call to Yusef, who told them a thing or two that wasn't in the codes. We broke this one up, Tony. That JK kid will come in really handy in the future. He's a genius – even if he is so spaceheaded at times I don't know what to do!"

Tony shrugged and agreed that JK wasn't at all easy to understand.

"We had two of the committee employees working on sensitive Crane projects," Tony suddenly said.

"Uh-oh! In very important spots?"

"Full clearance. I figured it would be a bad move to simply dump them, so I've reassigned them to less sensitive projects. Claimed productivity is down and I have to shuffle to pick it back up. I moved a few others around where it wouldn't matter. It's probably safe enough with the old understructure gone, but I'd hate to have them there if some new thing formed using the same idea."

"The people they placed were most certainly qualified. It's a pity to lose them."

"We'll use them elsewhere is all."

I spent a couple more hours on company business, then went to Len's office to tell him what we'd learned. Interpol had called and told him much the same thing. We went back to the labs to talk with Nora, George and Ed, then Len went back to work and I went home. Alma was in the cool house, so I went in to pot a few crosses that were overdue.

"Do you think it would be a good idea to cross this AM Tommie Hanes on the Gurkley?" Alma asked as I came in.

"McLellan's probably already did that. They did a lot of work with Gurkley."

"I didn't ask that. I asked if it would be a good idea."

"No. Gurkley's too dominant. All you get is more Gurkley."

"Oh, good! I'll cross them then!" she said with a leer.

Yep! Things are back to normal!

C. D. Moulton's works are available on most major outlets as printed or e-books. CD writes the CD Grimes, PI, mysteries, the Det. Lt. Nick Storie mysteries, the Clint Faraday mysteries, the Flight of the Maita science fiction series, books on orchid culture and many others of many types. Mystery, adventure, intrigue, science fiction, humor, fantasy, paranormal, mild erotica, and factual.